The Slipper Point Mystery

Augusta Huiell Seaman

ISBN: 1986586979

ISBN-13: 978-1986586979

Table of Contents

CHAPTER I

THE ENCOUNTER

SHE sat on the prow of a beached rowboat, digging her bare toes in the sand.

There were many other rowboats drawn up on the sandy edge of the river,—as many as twenty or thirty, not to speak of the green and red canoes lying on the shore, bottoms up, like so many strange insects. A large number of sailboats were also anchored near the shore or drawn up to the long dock that stretched out into the river.

For this was Carter's Landing, the only place on lovely little Manituck River where pleasure-boats could be hired. Beside the long dock there was, up a wide flight of steps a large pavilion where one could sit and watch the lights and shadows on the river and its many little activities. There were long benches and tables to accommodate picnic-parties and, in an inner room, a counter where candies, ice cream and soda-water were dispensed. And lastly, one part of the big pavilion was used as a dancing-floor where, afternoons and evenings, to the music of a violin and piano, merry couples whirled and circled.

Down on the sand was a signboard which said:

"Children Must Not Play in the Boats."

Nevertheless, she sat on the prow of one, this girl of fourteen, digging her bare toes aimlessly in the sand, and by her side on the prow-seat sat a tiny child of about three, industriously sucking the thumb of her right hand, while she pulled at a lock of her thick straight hair with her left. So she sat, saying nothing, but staring contentedly out over the water. The older girl wore a blue skirt and a soiled white middy-blouse. She had dark brown eyes and thick auburn hair, hanging down in a ropelike braid. Her face was somewhat freckled, and apart from her eyes and hair she was not particularly pretty.

The afternoon was hot, though it was only the early part of June, and there was no one else about except one or two helpers of the Landing. The girl stared moodily out over the blue river, and dug her bare toes deeper into the sand.

"Stop sucking your thumb, Genevieve!" she commanded suddenly, and the baby hastily removed the offending member from her mouth. But a moment later, when the older girl's attention was attracted elsewhere, she quietly slipped it back again.

Presently, from around the bend of the river, there slid into sight a red canoe, paddled vigorously by one person sitting in the stern. The girl in the prow of the rowboat sat up and stared intently at the approaching canoe.

"There it is," she announced to her younger sister. "The first canoe Dad's hired this season. Wonder who has it?" The baby made no reply and placidly continued to suck her thumb, her older sister being too absorbed to notice the forbidden occupation.

The canoe approached nearer, revealing its sole occupant to be a girl of fourteen or fifteen, clad in a dazzlingly white and distinctly tailored linen Russian blouse suit, with a pink satin tie, her curly golden hair surmounted by an immense bow of the same hue. She beached her canoe skilfully not six feet away from the rowboat of the occupied prow.

And as she stepped out, further details of her costume could be observed in fine white silk stockings and dainty patent leather pumps. Scarcely stopping to drag her canoe up further than a few inches on the sand, she hurried past the two in the rowboat and up the broad steps to the pavilion.

"You'd better drag up your canoe further," called out the barefooted girl. "It'll float away if you leave it like that."

"Oh, I'm coming right back!" replied the other. "I'm only stopping a moment to get some candy." She disappeared into the pavilion and was out again in two minutes, bearing a large box of candy, of the most expensive make boasted by Carter's Landing. Down the steps she tripped, and crossed the strip of sand toward her canoe. But in front of the occupied rowboat she stopped, drawn perhaps by the need of companionship on this beautiful but solitary afternoon.

"Have some?" she asked, proffering the open box of candy. The barefooted girl's eyes sparkled.

"Why, yes, thanks!" she answered, and gingerly helped herself to one small piece.

"Oh, take some more! There's plenty!" declared her companion, emptying fully a quarter of the box into her new friend's lap. "And give some to the baby." The younger child smiled broadly, removed her thumb from her mouth and began to munch ecstatically on a large piece of chocolate proffered by her sister.

"You're awfully kind," remarked the older girl between two bites, "but what'll your mother say?"

"Why, she won't care. She gave me the money and told me to go get it and amuse myself. It's awfully dull up at the hotel. It's so early in the season that there's almost nobody else there,—only two old ladies and a few men that come down at night,—besides Mother and myself. I hate going to the country so early, before things start, only Mother has been sick and needed the change right away. So here we are—and I'm as dull as dishwater and *so* lonesome! What's your name?"

The other girl had been drinking in all this information with such greedy interest that she scarcely heard or heeded the question which ended it. Without further questioning she realized that this new acquaintance was a guest at "The Bluffs," the one exclusive and fashionable hotel on the river. She at once became guiltily conscious of her own bare brown toes, still wriggling in the warm sand. She blamed herself fiercely for not taking the trouble to put on her shoes and stockings that afternoon. Up till this moment it had scarcely seemed worth while.

"Tell me, what's your name?" the girl in white and pink reiterated.

"Sarah," she answered, "but most every one calls me Sally. What's yours?"

"Doris Craig," was the reply and the girl of the bare toes unconsciously noted that "Doris" was an entirely fitting name for so dainty a creature. And somehow she dreaded to answer the question as to her own.

"My name's horrid," she added, "and I always did hate it. But baby's is pretty,—Genevieve. Mother named her that, 'cause Father had insisted that mine must be 'Sarah,' after his mother. She said she was going to have one pretty name in the family, anyway. Genevieve, take your thumb out of your mouth!"

"Why do you tell her to do that?" demanded Doris, curiously.

" 'Cause Mother says it'll make her mouth a bad shape if she keeps it up, and she told me it was up to me to stop it. You see I have Genevieve with me most of the time. Mother's so busy." But by this time, Doris's roving eye had caught the sign forbidding children to play in the boats.

"Do you see that?" she asked. "Aren't you afraid to be sitting around in that boat?"

"Huh!" exclaimed Sally scornfully. "That doesn't mean Genevieve and me."

"Why not?" cried Doris perplexedly.

" 'Cause we belong here. Captain Carter's our father. All these boats belong to him. Besides, it's so early in the season that it doesn't matter anyway. Even we don't do it much in July and August."

"Oh!" exclaimed Doris, a light beginning to break on her understanding. "Then that—er—lady up at the candy counter is your mother?" She referred to the breathlessly busy, pleasant, though anxious-faced woman who had sold her the candy.

"Yes. She's awfully busy all the time, 'cause she has to wait on the soda and candy and ice cream, and see that the freezer's working all right, and a lot of other things. In July and August we have to have girls from the village to help. We don't see much of her in the summer,—Genevieve and I. We just have to take care of ourselves. And that's Dad, down on the dock." She pointed to a tall, lanky, slouchily dressed man who was directing the lowering of a sail in one of the catboats.

"Yes, I know Captain Carter," averred Doris. "I hired this canoe of him."

"Did you go and hire a canoe—all by yourself?" inquired Sally, eyeing her very youthful new acquaintance with some wonder. "How did your mother come to let you?"

"Well, you see Mother's been awfully sick and she isn't at all well yet. Has to stay in bed a good deal of the day and just sits around on the veranda the rest of the time. *She* couldn't tend to things like that, so I've got used to doing them myself lately. I dress myself and fix my hair all by myself, without the least help from her,—which I couldn't do three months ago. I did it today. Don't you think I look all right?"

Again Sally flushed with the painful consciousness of her own unkempt appearance, especially her bare feet. "Oh, yes! You look fine," she acknowledged sheepishly. And then added, as a concession to her own attire:

"I hate to get all dressed up these hot days, 'specially when there's no one around. Mother often makes me during 'the season,' 'cause she says it looks bad for the Landing to see us children around so sloppy."

"My mother says," remarked Doris, "that one always feels better to be nicely and cleanly dressed, especially in the afternoons, if you can manage it. You feel so much more self-respecting. I often hate to bother to dress, too, but I always do it to please her."

Sally promptly registered the mental vow that she would hereafter array herself and Genevieve in clean attire every single afternoon, or perish in the attempt. But clothes was not a subject that ever interested Doris Craig for any length of time, so she soon switched to another.

"Can't you and the baby come out with me in my canoe for a while?" she suggested. "I'm so lonesome. And perhaps you know how to paddle. You could sit in the bow, and Genevieve in the middle."

"Yes, I know how to paddle," admitted Sally. To tell the truth she knew how to run every species of boat her father owned, not even omitting the steam launches. "But we can't take Genevieve in a canoe. She won't sit still enough and Mother has forbidden it. Let's go out in my rowboat instead. Dad lets me use old 45 for myself any time I want, except in the very rush season. It's kind of heavy and leaks a little, but I can row it all right." She indicated a boat far down at the end of the line.

"But I can't row!" exclaimed Doris. "I never learned because we've always had a canoe up at Lake Placid in the Adirondacks where we've usually gone."

"Oh, that doesn't matter," laughed Sally. "I can row the whole three. You sit in the stern with Genevieve, and I'll take you around the river to some places I warrant you've never seen."

Filled with the spirit of the new adventure, the two hurried along, bearing a somewhat reluctant Genevieve between them, and clambered into the boat numbered "45" at the end of the line. Doris seated herself in the stern with Genevieve and the box of candy. And the baby was soon shyly cuddling up to her and dipping her chubby little fist into the box at frequent intervals. Sally established herself in the bow rowing seat, pushed off with a skilful twist of her oars, and was soon swinging out into the tide with the short, powerful strokes of the native-born to Manituck.

It was a perfect June afternoon. The few other boats on the river were mainly those of the native fishermen treading for clams in the shallows, and one or two dipping sailboats. Overhead the fish-hawks sailed and plunged occasionally with a silver flash into the river. The warm scent of the pines was almost overpoweringly sweet, and a robin sang insistently on the farther shore. Even the thoughtless children were unconsciously swayed by the quiet beauty of the day and place.

"Do you know," commented Doris, "I like it here. Really I like it a lot better than any other place we've ever been. And I've only been here two days. Do you live here all the year round?"

"Yes, but it isn't half so nice in winter," said Sally; "though the skating's good when it's cold enough. But I get awfully tired of all this all the time. I'd love to live in New York a while. There's the island," she indicated. "You can see that from most anywhere on the river. It's pretty, but there isn't anything much interesting about it. I think I've explored every inch of this river 'cause I've so little else to do in the summer. Genevieve and I know more about it than the oldest inhabitant here, I reckon."

There was something about the way she made this last remark that aroused Doris's curiosity.

"Why do you say that?" she demanded. "Of course it's all lovely around here, and up above that bridge it seems rather wild. I went up there yesterday in the canoe. But what is there to 'know' about this river or its shores? There can't be anything very mysterious about a little New Jersey river like this."

"You wouldn't think so to look at it," said Sally, darkly. "Especially this lower part with just the Landing and the hotel and the summer bungalows along the shore. But above the bridge there in the wild part, things are different. Genevieve and I have poked about a bit, haven't we, Genevieve?" The baby nodded gravely, though it is doubtful if she understood much of her older sister's remark.

"Oh, *do* tell me what you've found?" cried Doris excitedly. "It all sounds so mysterious. I'm just crazy to hear. Can't you just give me a little hint about it, Sally?"

But the acquaintance was too new, and the mystery was evidently too precious for the other to impart just yet. She shook her head emphatically and replied:

"No, honestly I somehow don't want to. It's Genevieve's secret and mine. And we've promised each other we'd never tell any one about it. Haven't we, Genevieve?" The baby gravely nodded again, and Sally headed her boat for the wagon-bridge that crossed the upper part of the river.

CHAPTER II

THE ACQUAINTANCE RIPENS

DORIS said no more on the subject. She was too well-bred to persist in such a demand when it did not seem to be welcome. But though she promptly changed the subject and talked about other things, inwardly she had become transformed into a seething cauldron of curiosity.

Sally headed the boat for the draw in the bridge, and in another few moments they had passed from the quiet, well-kept, bungalow-strewn shores of the lower river, to the wild, tawny, uninhabited beauty of the upper. The change was very marked, and the wagon bridge seemed to be the dividing line.

"How different the river is up here," remarked Doris. "Not a house or a bungalow, or even a fisherman's shack in sight."

"It is," agreed Sally. And then, in an unusual burst of confidence, she added, "Do you know what I always think of when I pass through that bridge into this part of the river? It's from the 'Ancient Mariner':

" 'We were the first that ever burst

Into that silent sea.' "

Doris stared at her companion in amazement. How came this barefooted child of thirteen or fourteen, in a little, out-of-the-way New Jersey coast village to be quoting poetry? Where had she learned it? Doris's own father and mother were untiring readers of poetry and other literature, and they were bringing their daughter up in their footsteps. But surely, this village girl had never learned such things from *her* parents. Sally must have sensed the unspoken question.

"That's a long poem in a big book we have," she explained. "It has lovely pictures in it made by a man named Doré." (She pronounced it "Door.") "The book was one of my mother's wedding presents. It always lies on our parlor table. I don't believe any one else in our house has ever read it but Genevieve and me. I love it, and Genevieve likes to look at the pictures. Did you ever hear of that poem?"

"Oh, yes!" cried Doris. "My father has often read me to sleep with it, and we all love it. I'm so glad it is a favorite of yours. Do you like poetry?"

"That's about the only poem I know," acknowledged Sally, " 'cept the ones in the school readers—and they don't amount to much. That book's about the only one we have 'cept a Bible and a couple of novels. But I've learned the poem all by heart." She rowed on a way in silence, while Doris marvelled at the bookless condition of this lonely child and wondered how she could stand it. Not to have books and papers and magazines unnumbered was a state unheard of to the city child. She had brought half a trunkful with her, to help while away the time at Manituck. But before she could speak of it, Sally remarked:

"That's Huckleberry Heights,—at least I've named it that, 'cause Genevieve and I have picked quarts and quarts of huckleberries there." She pointed to a high, sandy bluff, overgrown at the top with scrub-oak, stunted pines and huckleberry bushes. "And that's Cranberry Creek," she went on, indicating a winding stream that emptied into the river nearby. " 'Way up that creek there's an old, deserted mill that's all falling to pieces. It's kind of interesting. Want to go sometime?"

"Oh, I'm crazy to!" cried Doris. "There's nothing I enjoy more than exploring things, and I've never had the chance to before. We've always gone to such fashionable places where everything's just spic and span and cut and dried, and nothing to do but what every one else does. I'm deathly sick of that sort of thing. Our doctor recommended Mother to come to this place because the sea and pine air would be so good for her. But he said it was wild, and different from the usual summer places, and I was precious glad of the change, I can tell you." There was something so sincere in Doris's manner that it won Sally over another point. After a few moments of silent rowing, she said:

"We're coming to a place, in a minute, that Genevieve and I like a lot. If you want, we can land there and get a dandy drink of water from a spring near the shore." Doris was flattered beyond words to be taken further into the confidence of this strange new acquaintance, and heartily assented. Around a bend of the river, they approached a point of land projecting out several hundred feet into the tide, its end terminating in a long, golden sandbar. Toward the shore, the land gently ascended in a pretty slope, crowned with velvety pines and cedars. The conformation of slope and trees gave the outjut of land a curious shape.

"Do you know what I call this point?" questioned Sally. Doris shook her head. "Well, you see what a queer shape it is when you look at it from the side. I've named it 'Slipper Point.' Doesn't it look like a slipper?"

"It certainly does," agreed Doris enthusiastically. "Why, you're a wonder at naming things, Sally." Her companion colored with pleasure, and beached the boat sharply on the sandbar. The three got out, put the anchor in the sand and clambered up the piny slope. At the top, the view up and down the river was enchanting, and the three sat down on the pine needles to regain their breath and rest. At length Sally suggested that they find the spring, and she led the way down the opposite side of the slope to a spot near the shore. Here, in a bower of branches, almost hidden from sight, a sparkling spring trickled down from a small cave of reddish clay, filled an old, moss-covered box, and rambled on down the sand into the river. Sally unearthed an old china cup from some hidden recess of her own, and Doris drank the most delicious water she had ever tasted.

But while Sally was drinking and giving Genevieve a share, Doris glanced at the little gold wrist-watch she wore.

"Gracious sakes!" she exclaimed. "It's nearly five o'clock and Mother'll begin to think I've tumbled into the river and drowned. She's always sure I'm going to do that some time. We must hurry back."

"All right," said Sally. "Jump into the boat and I'll have you home in a jiffy." They raced back to the boat, clambered into their former places, and were soon shooting down the river under the impetus of the tide and Sally's muscular strokes. The candy was by now all consumed. Genevieve cuddled down close to Doris, her thumb once more in her mouth, and went peacefully to sleep. The two other girls talked at intervals, but Sally was too busy pulling to waste much breath in conversation.

"I'll land you right at the hotel dock," she remarked, when at last they had come within sight of it. "Don't worry about your canoe. I'll bring that up myself, right after supper, and walk back."

"Thanks," said Doris gratefully. "That'll save me a lot of time." In another moment Sally had beached the boat on the shore directly in front of "The Bluffs," and Doris, gently disengaging the still sleeping Genevieve, hopped ashore. "I'll see you soon again, Sally," she said, "but I've got to just scamper now, I'm so worried about Mother." She raced away up the steps, breathless with fear lest her long absence had unduly upset her invalid mother, and Sally again turned her boat out into the tide.

After supper that evening, Doris sat out at the end of the hotel pier, watching the gradual approach of sunset behind the island. Her mind was still full of the afternoon's encounter, and she wondered vaguely whether she should see more of the strange village child, so ignorant about many things, so careless about her personal appearance, who could yet quote such a wonderful poem as "The Ancient Mariner" in appropriate places and seemed to be acquainted with some queer mystery about the river. Presently she noticed a red canoe slipping into sight around a bend, and in another moment recognized Sally in the stern.

There was no Genevieve with her this time. And to Doris's wondering eyes, the change in her appearance was quite amazing. No longer barefooted, she was clothed in neat tan stockings and buttoned shoes. Added to that, she boasted a pretty, well-fitting blue serge skirt and dainty blouse. But the only jarring note was a large pink bow of hideous hue, a patent imitation of the one Doris wore, balanced on her beautiful bronze hair. She managed the canoe with practiced ease, and waved her hand at Doris from afar.

"Here's your canoe!" she called, as Doris hurried down the long dock to meet her on the shore. And as they met, Doris remarked:

"It's early yet. How would you like to paddle around a while? I'll run in and ask Mother if I may." Again Sally flushed with pleasure as she assented, and when Doris had rushed back and seated herself in the bow of the canoe, they pushed out into the peaceful tide, wine-colored in the approaching sunset. But the evening was too beautiful for strenuous paddling. Doris soon shipped her paddle and, skilfully turning' in her seat, faced Sally.

"Let's not go far," she suggested, "let's just drift—and talk." Sally herself was privately only too willing. Dipping her paddle only occasionally to keep from floating in shore, she nodded another approving assent. But her country unaccustomedness to conversation held her tongue-tied for a time.

"Where's Genevieve?" demanded Doris.

"Oh, I put her to bed at half-past six most always," said Sally. "She's usually so sleepy she can't even finish her supper. But I miss her evenings. She's a lot of company for me."

"She's a darling!" agreed Doris. "I just love the way she cuddles up to me, and she looks so—so appealing when she tucks that little thumb in her mouth. But, Sally, will you forgive my saying it?—you look awfully nice tonight." Sally turned absolutely scarlet in her appreciation of this compliment. Truth to tell, she had spent quite an hour over her toilet when Genevieve had been put to bed, and had even gone flying to the village to purchase with her little hoard of pocket-money the pink ribbon for her hair.

"But I wonder if you'd mind my saying something else," went on Doris, eyeing her companion critically. "You've got the loveliest colored hair I ever saw, but I think you ought never to wear any colored ribbon but black on it. Pink's all right for very light or very dark people, but not for any one with your lovely shade. You don't mind my saying that, do you? Sometimes other people can tell what looks best on you so much better than you can yourself."

"Oh, no. I don't mind—and thank you for telling me," stammered Sally, in an agony of combined delight that this dainty new friend should approve her appearance and shame that she had made such an error of judgment in selecting the pink ribbon. Mentally, too, she was calculating just how long it would take her to save, from the stray pennies her mother occasionally gave her, enough to purchase the suggested black one. While she was figuring it out, Doris had something else to suggest:

"Sally, let's be good friends. Let's see each other every day. I'm awfully lonesome when I'm not with Mother,—even more so than you, because you've got Genevieve. I expect to stay here all summer, and they say there are very few young folks coming to 'The Bluffs.' It's mostly older people there, because the younger ones like the hotels on the ocean best. So things won't be much better for me, even during the season. Can't we be good friends and see each other a lot, and have a jolly time on the river,—you and Genevieve and I?"

The appeal was one that Sally could scarcely have resisted, even had she not herself yearned for the same thing. "It—it would be fine!" she acknowledged, shyly. "I'm—I'm awfully glad—if you want to."

They drifted about idly a while longer, discussing a trip for the next morning, in which Sally proposed to show her new friend the deserted mill, up Cranberry Creek. And Doris announced that she was going to learn to row, so that the whole burden of that task might not fall on Sally.

"But now I must go in," she ended. "It's growing dark and Mother will worry. But you be here in the morning at half-past nine with your boat, if we'd better not take the canoe on account of Genevieve, and we'll have a jolly day."

Not once during all this time, had there been the least reference to the mysterious hint of Sally's during the earlier afternoon. But this was not at all because Doris had forgotten it. She was, to tell the truth, even more curious about it than ever. Her vivid imagination had been busy with it ever since, weaving all sorts of strange and fantastic fancies about the suggestion. Did the river have a mystery? What could its nature be, and how had Sally discovered it? Did any one else know? The deepening shadows on the farther shore added the last touch to her busy speculations. They suggested possibilities of every hue and kind. But not for worlds would she have had Sally guess how ardently she longed for its revelation. Sally should tell her in good time, or not at all, if she were so inclined: never because she (Doris) had *asked* to be admitted to this precious secret.

They beached the canoe, still talking busily about the morrow's plans, and together hauled it up in the sea-grass and turned it bottom upward. And then Sally prepared to take her departure. But after she had said good-bye, she still lingered uncertainly, as if she had something else on her mind. It was only when she had turned to walk away across the beach, that she suddenly wheeled and ran up to Doris once more.

"I—I want to tell you something," she hesitated. "I—perhaps—sometime I'll tell you more, but—the *secret*—Genevieve's and mine—is up on Slipper Point!"

And before Doris could reply, she was gone, racing away along the darkening sand.

CHAPTER III

SALLY CAPITULATES

IT was the beginning of a close friendship. For more than a week thereafter, the girls were constantly together. They met every morning by appointment at the hotel dock, where Sally always rowed up in "45," and Genevieve never failed to be the third member of the party. The canoe was quite neglected, except occasionally, in the evening, when Doris and Sally alone paddled about in her for a short time before sunset, or just after. Sally introduced Doris to every spot on the river, every shady bay and inlet or creek that was of the slightest interest. They explored the deserted mill, gathered immense quantities of water-lilies in Cranberry Creek, penetrated for several miles up the windings of the larger creek that was the source of the river, camped and picnicked for the day on the island, and paddled barefooted all one afternoon in the rippling water across its golden bar.

Beside that, they deserted the boat one day and walked to the ocean and back, through the scented aisles of an interminable pine forest. On the ocean beach they explored the wreck of a schooner cast up on the sand in the storm of a past winter, and played hide-and-seek with Genevieve among the billowy dunes. But in all this time neither had once mentioned the subject of the secret on Slipper Point. Doris, though consumed with impatient curiosity, was politely waiting for Sally to make any further disclosures she might choose, and Sally was waiting for—she knew not quite what! But had she realized it, she would have known she was waiting for some final proof that her confidence in her new friend was not misplaced.

Not even yet was she absolutely certain that Doris was as utterly friendly as she seemed. Though she scarcely acknowledged it to herself, she was dreading and fearing that this new, absorbing friendship could not last. When the summer had advanced and there were more companions of Doris's own kind in Manituck, it would all come to an end. She would be forgotten or neglected, or, perhaps even snubbed for more suitable acquaintances. How could it be otherwise? And how could she disclose her most precious secret to one who might later forsake her and even impart it to some one else? No, she would wait.

In the meantime, while Doris was growing rosy and brown in the healthful outdoor life she was leading with Sally, Sally herself was imbibing new ideas and thoughts and interests in long, ecstatic draughts. Chief among all these were the books—the wonderful books and magazines that Doris had brought with her in a seemingly endless amount. Sometimes Doris could scarcely extract a word from Sally during a whole long morning or afternoon, so deeply absorbed was she in some volume loaned her by her obliging friend. And Doris also knew that Sally sat up many a night, devouring by candle-light the book she wanted to return next day—so that she might promptly replace it by another!

One thing puzzled Doris,—the curious choice of books that seemed to appeal to Sally. She read them all with equal avidity and appeared to enjoy them all at the time, but some she returned to for a second reading, and one in particular she demanded again and again. Doris's own choice lay in the direction of Miss Alcott's works and "Little Lord Fauntleroy" and her favorites among Dickens. Sally took these all in with the rest, but she borrowed a second time the books of a more adventurous type, and to Doris's constant wonder, declared Stevenson's "Treasure Island" to be her favorite among them all. So frequently did she borrow this, that Doris finally gave her the book for her own, much to Sally's amazement and delight.

"Why do you like 'Treasure Island' best?" Doris asked her point-blank, one day. Sally's manner immediately grew a trifle reserved.

"Because—because," she stammered, "it is like—like something—oh! I can't just tell you right now, Doris. Perhaps I will some day." And Doris said no more, but put the curious remark away in her mind to wonder over.

"It's something connected with her secret—that I'm sure!" thought Doris. "I do wish she felt like telling me, but until she does, I'll try not even to think about it."

But, all unknown to Doris, the time of her final testing, in Sally's eyes, was rapidly approaching. Sally herself, however, had known of it and thought over it for a week or more. About the middle of June, there came every year to the "Bluffs" a certain party of young folks, half a dozen or more in number, with their parents, to stay till the middle of

July, when they usually left for the mountains. They were boys and girls of about Doris's age or a trifle older, rollicking, fun-loving, a little boisterous, perhaps, and on the go from morning till night. They spent their mornings at the ocean bathing-beach, their afternoons steaming up and down the river in the fastest motor-boat available, and their evenings dancing in the hotel parlor when they could find any one to play for them. Sally had known them by sight for several years, though never once, in all that time, had they so much as deigned to notice her existence.

"If Doris deserts me for them," she told herself, "then I'll be mighty glad I never told her my secret. Oh, I do wonder what she'll do when they come!"

And then they came. Sally knew of their arrival that evening, when they rioted down to the Landing to procure the fastest launch her father rented. And she waited, inwardly on tenterhooks of anxiety, for the developments of the coming days. But, to her complete surprise, nothing happened. Doris sought her company as usual, and for a day or two never even mentioned the presence of the newcomers. At last Sally could bear it no longer.

"How do you like the Campbells and Hobarts who are at your hotel now?" she inquired one morning.

"Why, they're all right," said Doris indifferently, feathering her oars with the joy of a newly-acquired accomplishment.

"But you don't seem to go around with them," ventured Sally uncertainly.

"Oh, they tire me to death, they're so rackety!" yawned Doris. "I like fun and laughing and joking and shouting as well as the next person—once in a while. But I can't stand it for steady diet. It's a morning, noon and night performance with them. They've invited me to go with them a number of times, and I will go once in a while, so as not to seem unsociable, but much of it would bore me to death. By the way, Sally, Mother told me to ask you to come to dinner with us tonight, if you care to. She's very anxious to meet you, for I've told her such a lot about you. Do you think your mother will allow you to come?"

Sally turned absolutely scarlet with the shock of surprise and joy this totally unexpected invitation caused her.

"Why—yes—er—that is, I think so. Oh, I'm sure of it! But, Doris, do you *really* want me? I'm—well, I'm only Sally Carter, you know," she stammered.

"Why, of course I want you!" exclaimed Doris, opening her eyes wide with surprise. "I shouldn't have asked you if I hadn't." And so it was settled. Sally was to come up that afternoon, for once without Genevieve, and have dinner at "The Bluffs" with the Craigs. She spent an agonized two hours making her toilet for the occasion, assisted by her anxious mother, who could scarcely fathom the reason for so unprecedented an invitation. When she was arrayed in the very best attire she owned (and a very creditable appearance she made, since she had adopted some of Doris's well-timed hints), her mother kissed her, bade her "mind how she used her knife and fork," and she set out for the hotel, joyful on one score, but thoroughly uncomfortable on many others.

But she forgot much of her agitation in the meeting with Mrs. Craig, a pale, lovely, golden-haired woman of the gentlest and most winning manner in the world. In five minutes she had put the shy, awkward village girl completely at her ease, and the three were soon conversing as unrestrainedly as if the mother of Doris was no more than their own age. But Sally could easily divine, from her weakness and pallor, how ill Mrs. Craig had been, and how far from strong she still was.

Dinner at their own cosy little table was by no means the ordeal Sally had expected, and when it was over Mrs. Craig retired to her room and Sally and Doris went out to sit for a while on the broad veranda. It was here that Doris passed the final test that Sally had set for her. There approached the sound of trooping footsteps and laughing voices, and in another moment, the entire Campbell-Hobart clan clattered by.

"Hello, Doris!" they greeted her. "Coming in to dance tonight?"

"I don't know," answered Doris. "Have you met my friend, Sally Carter?" And she made all the introductions with unconcerned, easy grace. The Campbell-Hobart faction stared. They knew Sally Carter perfectly well by sight, and all about who she was. What on earth was she doing here—at "The Bluffs"? A number of them murmured some indistinct rejoinder and one of them, in the background, audibly giggled. Sally heard the giggle and flushed painfully. But Doris was superbly indifferent to it all.

"Do you dance, Sally?" she inquired, and Sally stammered that she did not.

"Then we'll go down to the river and paddle about awhile," went on Doris. "It's much nicer than stampeding about that hot parlor." The Campbell-Hobart crowd melted away. "Come on, Sally!" said Doris, and, linking arms with her new friend, she strolled down the steps to the river, without alluding, by so much as a single syllable, to the rudeness of that noisy, thoughtless group.

And in the heart of Sally Carter there sprang into being such an absolute idolatry of adoration for this glorious new girl friend that she was ready to lie down and die for her at a moment's notice. The last barrier, the last doubt, was swept completely away. And, as they drifted about in the fading after-glow, Sally remarked, apropos of nothing:

"If you like, we'll go up to Slipper Point tomorrow, and—I'll show you—that secret!"

"Oh, Sally," breathed Doris in an awestruck whisper, "will you—*really*?"

CHAPTER IV

ON SLIPPER POINT

IT would be exaggeration to say that Doris slept, all told, one hour during the ensuing night. She napped at intervals, to be sure, but hour after hour she tossed about in her bed, in the room next to her mother, pulling out her watch every twenty minutes or so, and switching on the electric light to ascertain the time. Never in all her life had a night seemed so long. Would the morning ever come, and with it the revelation of the strange secret Sally knew?

Like many girls of her age, and like many older folks too, if the truth were known, Doris loved above all things, *a mystery*. Into her well-ordered and regulated life there had never entered one or even the suspicion of one. And since her own life was so devoid of this fascination, she had gone about for several years, speculating in her own imagination about the lives of others, and wondering if mystery ever entered into *their* existences. But not until her meeting with little Sally Carter, had there been even the faintest suggestion of such a thing. And now, at last—! She pulled out her watch and switched on her light for the fortieth time. Only quarter to five. But through her windows she could see the faint dawn breaking over the river, so she rose softly, dressed, and sat down to watch the coming of day.

At nine o'clock she was pacing nervously up and down the beach. And when old "45" at last grated on the sand, she hopped in with a glad cry, kissed and hugged Genevieve, who was devoting her attention to her thumb, in the stern seat, as usual, and sank down in the vacant rowing-seat, remarking to Sally:

"Hello, dear! I'm awfully glad you've come!" This remark may not seem to express very adequately her inward state of excitement but she had resolved not to let Sally see how tremendously anxious she was.

The trip to Slipper Point was a somewhat silent one. Neither of the girls seemed inclined to conversation and, besides that, there was a stiff head-wind blowing and the pulling was difficult. When they had beached the boat, at length, on the golden sandbar of Slipper Point, Doris only looked toward Sally and said:

"So you're going to show me at last, dear?" But Sally hesitated a moment.

"Doris," she began, "this is my secret—and Genevieve's—and I never thought I'd tell any one about it. It's the only secret I ever had worth anything, but I'm going to tell you,—well, because I—I think so much of you. Will you solemnly promise—cross your heart—that you'll never tell any one?"

Doris gazed straight into Sally's somewhat troubled eyes. "I don't need to 'cross my heart,' Sally. I just give you my word of honor I won't, unless sometime you wish it. I've not breathed a word of the fact that you *had* a secret, even to Mother. And I've never kept anything from her before." And this simple statement completely satisfied Sally.

"Come on, then," she said. "Follow Genevieve and me, and we'll give you the surprise of your life."

She grasped her small sister's hand and led the way, and Doris obediently followed. To her surprise, however, they did not scramble up the sandy pine-covered slope as usual, but picked their way, instead, along the tiny strip of beach on the farther side of the point where the river ate into the shore in a great, sweeping cove. After trudging along in this way for nearly a quarter of a mile, Sally suddenly struck up into the woods through a deep little ravine. It was a wild scramble through the dense underbrush and over the boughs of fallen pine trees. Sally and Genevieve, more accustomed to the journey, managed to keep well ahead of Doris, who was scratching her hands freely and doing ruinous damage to her clothes plunging through the thorny tangle. At last the two, who were a distance of not more than fifty feet ahead of her, halted, and Sally called out:

"Now stand where you are, turn your back to us and count ten—slowly. Don't turn round and look till you've finished counting." Doris obediently turned her back, and slowly and deliberately "counted ten." Then she turned about again to face them.

To her complete amazement, there was not a trace of them to be seen!

Thinking they had merely slipped down and hidden in the undergrowth to tease her, she scrambled to the spot where they had stood. But they were not there. She had, moreover, heard no sound of their progress, no snapping, cracking or breaking of branches, no swish of trailing through the vines and high grass. They could not have advanced twenty feet in any direction, in the short time she had been looking away from them. Of both these facts she was certain. Yet they had disappeared as completely as if the earth had opened and swallowed them. Where, in the name of all mystery, could they be?

Doris stood and studied the situation for several minutes. But, as they were plainly nowhere in her vicinity, she presently concluded she must have been mistaken about their not having had time to get further away, and determined to hunt them up.

So away she pursued her difficult quest, becoming constantly more involved in the thick undergrowth and more scratched and dishevelled every moment, till at length she stood at the top of the bluff. From this point she could see in every direction, but not a vestige of Sally or Genevieve appeared. More bewildered than ever, Doris clambered back to the spot where she had last seen them. And, as there was plainly now no other course, she stood where she was and called aloud:

"Sally! Sal—ly! I give it up. Where in the world are you?"

There was a low, chuckling laugh directly behind her, and, whirling about, she beheld Sally's laughing face peeping out from an aperture in the tangled growth that she was positive she had not noticed there before.

"Come right in!" cried Sally. "And I won't keep it a secret any longer. Did you guess it was anything like this?"

She pushed a portion of the undergrowth back a little farther and Doris scrambled in through the opening. No sooner was she within than Sally closed the opening with a swift motion and they were all suddenly plunged into inky darkness.

"Wait a moment," she commanded, "and I'll make a light." Doris heard her fumbling for something; then the scratch of a match and the flare of a candle. With an indrawn breath of wonder, Doris looked about her.

"Why, it's a room!" she gasped. "A little room all made right in the hillside. How did it ever come here? How did you ever find it?"

It was indeed the rude semblance of a room. About nine feet square and seven high, its walls, floor and ceiling were finished in rough planking of some kind of timber, now covered in the main with mold and fungus growths. Across one end was a low wooden structure evidently meant for a bed, with what had once been a hard straw mattress on it. There was likewise a rudely constructed chair and a small table on which were the rusted remains of a tin platter, knife and spoon. There was also a metal candle-stick in which was the candle recently lit by Sally. It was a strange, weird little scene in the dim candle-light, and for a time Doris could make nothing of its riddle.

"What *is* it? What does it all mean, Sally?" she exclaimed, gazing about her with awestruck eyes.

"I don't know much more about it than you do," Sally averred. "But I've done some guessing!" she ended significantly.

"But how did you ever come to discover it?" cried Doris, off on another tack. "I could have searched Slipper Point for years and never have come across *this*."

"Well, it was just an accident," Sally admitted. "You see, Genevieve and I haven't much to do most of the time but roam around by ourselves, so we've managed to poke into most of the places along the shore, the whole length of this river, one time and another. It was last fall when we discovered this. We'd climbed down here one day, just poking around looking for beach-plums and things, and right about here I caught my foot in a vine and went down on my face plumb right into that lot of vines and things. I threw out my hands to catch myself, and instead of coming against the sand and dirt as I'd expected, something gave way, and when I looked there was nothing at all there but a hole.

"Of course, I poked away at it some more, and found that there was a layer of planking back of the sand. That seemed mighty odd, so I pushed the vines away and banged some more at the opening, and it suddenly gave way because the boards had got rotten, I guess, and—I found *this*!"

Doris sighed ecstatically. "What a perfectly glorious adventure! And what did you do then?"

"Well," went on Sally simply, "although I couldn't make very much out of what it all was, I decided that we'd keep it for our secret,—Genevieve and I—and we wouldn't let another soul know about it. So we pulled the vines and things over the opening the best we could, and we came up next day and brought some boards and a hammer and nails—and a candle. Then I fixed up the rotten boards of this opening,—you see it works like a door, only the outside is covered with vines and things so you'd never see it,—and I got an old padlock from Dad's boathouse and I screwed it on the outside so's I could lock it up besides, and covered the padlock with vines and sand. Nobody'd ever dream there was such a place here, and I guess nobody ever has, either. That's my secret!"

"But, Sally," exclaimed Doris, "how did it ever come here to begin with? Who made it? It must have some sort of history."

"There you've got *me*!" answered Sally.

"Some one must have stayed here," mused Doris, half to herself. "And, what's more, they must have *hidden* here, or why should they have taken such trouble to keep it from being discovered?"

"Yes, they've hidden here, right enough," agreed Sally. "It's the best hiding place any one ever had, I should say. But the question is, what did they hide here for?"

"And also," added Doris, "if they were hiding, how could they make such a room as this, all finished with wooden walls, without being seen doing it? Where did they get the planks?"

"Do you know what that timber is?" asked Sally.

"Why, of course not," laughed Doris. "How should I?"

"Well, I do," said her companion. "I know something about lumber because Dad builds boats and he's shown me. I scratched the mold off one place,—here it is,—and I discovered that this planking is real seasoned cedar like they build the best boats of. And do you know where I think it was got? It came from some wrecked vessel down on the beach. There are plenty of them cast up, off and on, and always have been."

"But gracious!" cried Doris, "how was it got here?"

"Don't ask me!" declared Sally. "The beach is miles away."

They stood for some moments in silence, each striving to piece together the story of this strange little retreat from the meagre facts they saw about them. At last Doris spoke.

"Sally," she asked, "was this all you ever found here? Was there absolutely nothing else?" Sally started, as if surprised at the question and hesitated a moment.

"No," she acknowledged finally. "There *was* something else. I wasn't going to tell you right away, but I might as well now. I found this under the mattress of the bed."

She went over to the straw pallet, lifted it, searched a moment and, turning, placed something in Doris's hands.

CHAPTER V

MYSTERY

DORIS received the object from Sally and stood looking at it as it lay in her hands. It was a small, square, very flat tin receptacle of some kind, rusted and moldy, and about six inches long and wide. Its thickness was probably not more than a quarter of an inch.

"What in the world is it?" she questioned wonderingly.

"Open it and see!" answered Sally. Doris pried it open with some difficulty. It contained only a scrap of paper which fitted exactly into its space. The paper was brown with age and stained beyond belief. But on its surface could be dimly discerned a strange and inexplicable design.

"Of *all* things!" breathed Doris in an awestruck voice. "This certainly is a mystery, Sally. What *do* you make of it?"

"I don't make anything of it," Sally averred. "That's just the trouble. I can't imagine what it means. I've studied and studied over it all winter, and it doesn't seem to mean a single thing."

It was indeed a curious thing, this scrap of stained, worn paper, hidden for who knew how many years in a tin box far underground. For the riddle on the paper was this:

3	6	1	4	5	2	
f	m	u	o	3	s	5
x	d	5	y	t	g	1
e	v	2	h	9	k	4
6	a	g	l	p	7	3
b	i	o	r	1	j	6
r	4	w	n	z	c	2

"Well, I give it up!" declared Doris, after she had stared at it intently for several more silent moments. "It's the strangest puzzle I ever saw. But, do you know, Sally, I'd like to take it home and study it out at my leisure. I always was crazy about puzzles, and I'd just enjoy working over this, even if I never made anything out of it. Do you think it would do any harm to remove it from here?"

"I don't suppose it would," Sally replied, "but somehow I don't like to change anything here or take anything away even for a little while. But you can study it out all you wish, though, for I made a copy of it a good while ago, so's I could study it myself. Here it is." And Sally pulled from her pocket a duplicate of the strange design, made in her own handwriting.

At this point, Genevieve suddenly became restless and, clinging to Sally's skirts, demanded to "go and play in the boat."

"She doesn't like to stay in here very long," explained Sally.

"Well, I don't wonder!" declared Doris. "It's dark and dreary and weird. It makes me feel kind of curious and creepy myself. But, oh! it's a glorious secret, Sally,—the strangest and most wonderful I ever heard of. Why, it's a regular *adventure* to have found such a thing as this. But let's go out and sit in the boat and let Genevieve paddle. Then we can talk it all over and puzzle this out."

Sally returned the tin box and its contents to the hiding-place under the mattress. Then she blew out the candle, remarking as she did so that she'd brought a lot of candles and matches and always kept them there. In the pall of darkness that fell on them, she groped for the entrance, pushed it open and they all scrambled out into the daylight. After that she padlocked the opening and buried the key in the sand nearby and announced herself ready to return to the boat.

During the remainder of that sunny morning they sat together in the stern of the boat, golden head and auburn one bent in consultation over the strange combination of letters and figures, while Genevieve, barefooted, paddled in silent ecstasy in the shallow water rippling over the bar.

"Sally," exclaimed Doris, at length, suddenly straightening and looking her companion in the eyes, "I believe you have some idea about all this that you haven't told me yet! Several remarks you've dropped make me think so. Now, honestly, haven't you? What *do* you believe is the secret of this cave and this queer jumble of letters and things, anyway?"

Sally, thus faced, could no longer deny the truth. "Yes," she acknowledged, "there *is* something I've thought of, and the more I think of it, the surer I am. And something that's happened since I knew you, has made me even surer yet." She paused, and Doris, wild with impatience, demanded, "Well?"

"*It's pirates!*" announced Sally, slowly and distinctly.

"*What?*" cried Doris, jumping to her feet. "Impossible! There's no such thing, nowadays."

"I didn't say 'nowadays,' " remarked Sally, calmly. "I think it *was* pirates, then, if that suits you better."

Doris sank down in her seat again in amazed silence. "A pirate cave!" she breathed at last. "I do believe you're right, Sally. What else *could* it be? But where's the treasure, then? Pirates always had some around, didn't they? And that cave would be the best kind of a place to keep it."

"That's what this tells," answered Sally, pointing to the scrap of paper. "I believe it's buried somewhere, and this is the secret plan that tells where it is. If we could only puzzle it out, we'd find the treasure."

A great light suddenly dawned on Doris. "*Now* I know," she cried, "why you were so crazy over 'Treasure Island.' It was all about pirates, and there was a secret map in it. You thought it might help you to puzzle out this. Wasn't that it?"

"Yes," said Sally, "that was it, of course. I was wondering if you'd guess it. I've got the book under the bow seat of the boat now. Let's compare the things." She lifted the seat, found the book, which fell open of its own accord, Doris noticed, at the well-known chart of that well-loved book. They laid their own riddle beside it.

"But this is entirely different," declared Doris. "That one of 'Treasure Island' is a map or chart, with the hills and trees and everything written plainly on it. This is nothing but a jumble of letters and figures in little squares, and doesn't make the slightest sense, no matter how you turn or twist it."

"I don't care," insisted Sally. "I suppose all secret charts aren't alike. I believe if we only knew how to work this one, it would certainly direct us straight to the place where that treasure is buried."

So positive was she, that Doris could not help but be impressed. "But pirates lived a long time ago," she objected, "and I don't believe there were ever any pirates around this place, anyway. I thought they were mostly down around Cuba and the southern parts of this country."

"Don't you believe it!" cried Sally. "I've heard lots of the old fishermen about here tell how there used to be pirates right along this coast, and how they used to come in these little rivers once in a while and bury their stuff and then go out for more. Why there was one famous one they call 'Captain Kidd,' and they say he buried things all about here, but mostly on the ocean beach. My father says there used to be an old man (he's dead now) right in our village, and he was just sure he could find some buried treasure, and he was always digging around on the beach and in the woods near the ocean. Folks thought he was just kind of crazy. But once he really did find something, way down deep, that looked like it might have been the bones of a skeleton, and a few queer coins and things all mixed up with them. And then every one went wild and began digging for dear life, too, for a while, but they never found anything more, so gradually they left off and forgot it."

Doris was visibly stirred by this curious story. After all, why should it not be so? Why, perhaps could not *they* be on the right track of the buried treasure of pirate legend? The more she thought it over, the more possible it became. And the fascination of such a possibility held her spellbound.

"Yes," she agreed, "I do believe you're right, Sally. And now that I look it over, these letters and numbers might easily be the key to it all, if we can only work it out. Oh, I never heard of anything so wonderful happening to two girls like ourselves before! Thank you, a million times, Sally, for sharing this perfectly marvelous secret with me."

"I do believe I'm enjoying it a great deal better myself, now that I've told you," answered Sally. "I didn't think it could be so before I did. And if we ever discover what it all means——"

"Why, precious!" interrupted Doris, turning to Genevieve, who all unnoticed had come to lean disconsolately against the side of the boat, her thumb tucked pathetically in her mouth, her eyes half tearful. "What's the matter?"

"I'm hung'y and s'eepy!" moaned Genevieve. With a guilty start, Doris gazed at her wrist watch. It was nearly one o'clock.

"Merciful goodness! Mother will be frantic!" she exclaimed. "It's lunch-time now, and we're way up here. And just see the way I look!" She was indeed a scratched, grimy and tattered object. "Whatever will I tell her?" They scrambled to their oars and were out in the river before Sally answered this question.

"Can't you tell her you were exploring up on Slipper Point?"

"Yes," agreed Doris. "That is the real truth. And she never minds if I get mussed and dirty, as long as I've enjoyed myself in some way that's all right. But I hope I haven't worried her by being so late."

They rowed on in mad, breathless haste, passed the wagon-bridge, and came at last in sight of the hotel. But as they beached the boat, and Doris scrambled out, she said in parting:

"I've been thinking, all the way down, about that secret map, or whatever it is, and I have a new idea about it. I'll tell you tomorrow morning. This afternoon I've promised to go for a drive with Mother."

CHAPTER VI

WORKING AT THE RIDDLE

BUT Doris did not have an opportunity to communicate her idea on the following morning, nor for several days after that. A violent three or four days' northeaster had set in, and for forty-eight hours after their expedition to Slipper Point, the river was swept by terrific gales and downpouring sheets of rain. Doris called up Sally by telephone from the hotel, on the second day, for she knew that Sally would very likely be at the Landing, where there was a telephone connection.

"Can't you get well wrapped up and come up here to see me a while?" she begged. "I'd go to you, but Mother won't let me stir out in this awful downpour."

"I could, I s'pose, but, honestly, I'd rather not," replied Sally, doubtfully. "I don't much like to come up to the hotel. I guess you know why." Doris did know.

"But you can come up to my room, and we'll be alone there," she suggested. "I've so much I want to talk to you about. I've thought of something else,—a dandy scheme." The plan sorely tempted Sally, but a new thought caused her to refuse once more.

"I'd have to bring Genevieve," she reminded Doris, "and she mightn't behave, and—well, I really guess I'd better not."

"Perhaps tomorrow will be nice again," ended Doris, hopefully, as she hung up the receiver.

But the morrow was not at all "nice." On the contrary, it was, if anything, worse than ever. After the morning mail had come, however, Doris excitedly called up Sally again.

"You simply must come up here, if it's only for a few minutes!" she told her. "I've something awfully important that I just must talk to you about and show you." The "show you" was what convinced Sally.

"All right," she replied. "I'll come up for half an hour. I'll leave Genevieve with Mother. But I can't stay any longer."

She came, not very long after, and Doris rushed to meet her from the back porch, for she had walked up the road. Removing her dripping umbrella and mackintosh, Doris led her up to her room, whispering excitedly:

"I don't know what you'll think of what I've done, Sally, but one thing I'm certain of. It can't do any harm and it may do some good."

"What in the world is it?" questioned Sally, wonderingly.

Doris drew her into her own room and shut the door. The communicating door to her mother's room was also shut, so they were quite alone. When Sally was seated, Doris laid a bulky bundle in her lap.

"What is it?" queried Sally, wide-eyed, wondering what all this could have to do with their mystery.

"I'll tell you," said Doris. "If it hadn't been for this awful storm, I'd have told you and asked you about it next morning, but I didn't want to over the 'phone. So I just took things in my own hands, and here's the result." Sally was more bewildered than ever.

"What's the result?"

"Why, just this," went on Doris. "That night, after we'd been to Slipper Point, I lay awake again the longest time, thinking and thinking. And suddenly a bright idea occurred to me. You know, whenever I'm worried or troubled or puzzled, I always go to Father and ask his advice. I can go to Mother too, but she's so often ill and miserable, and I've got into the habit of not bothering her with things. But Father's always ready, and he's never failed me yet. So I got to wondering how I could get some help from him in this affair without, of course, his suspecting anything about the secret part of it. And then, all of a sudden, I thought of—*books*! There must be *some* books that would help us,—books that would give us some kind of information that might lead to a clue.

"So next morning, very first thing, I sent a special delivery letter to Father asking him to send me down *at once* any books he could find about *pirates* and such things. And, bless his heart, he sent me down a whole bundle of them that just got here this morning!"

Sally eyed them in a sort of daze. "But—but won't your father guess just what we're up to?" she ventured, dubiously. "He will ask you what you want them for, won't he?"

"No, indeed," cried Doris. "That's just the beauty of Father. He'd never ask me *why* I want them in a hundred years. If I choose to explain to him, all right, and if I don't he knows that's all right too, for he trusts me absolutely, not to do anything wrong. So, when he comes down, as I expect he will in a week or so, he'll probably say, 'Pirates all right, daughter?' and that's all there'll be to it." Sally was at last convinced, though she marvelled inwardly at this quite wonderful species of father.

"But now, let's look at the books," went on Doris. "I'm perfectly certain we'll find something in them that's going to give us a lift." She unwrapped the bundle and produced three volumes. One, a very large one, was called "The Book of Buried Treasure." Another, "Pirates and Buccaneers of Our Own Coasts," and, last but not least, "The Life of Captain Kidd." Sally's eyes fairly sparkled, especially at the last, and they hurriedly consulted together as to who should take which books first. At length it was decided that Sally take the "Buried Treasure Book," as it was very bulky, and Doris would go over the other two. Then they would exchange. This ought to keep them fully occupied till fair weather set in again, after which, armed with so much valuable information, they would again tackle their problem on its own ground—at Slipper Point.

It was two days later when they met again. There had not been an opportunity to exchange the books, but on the first fair morning Sally and Genevieve rowed up in "45," and Doris leaped in exclaiming:

"Let's go right up to Slipper Point. I believe I've got on the track of something—at last! What have you discovered, Sally?"

"Nothing at all,—just nothing," declared Sally rather discouragingly. "It was an awfully interesting book, though. I just devoured it. But it didn't tell a thing that would help us out. And I've made up my mind, since reading it, that we might as well give up any idea of Captain Kidd having buried anything around here. That book said he never buried a thing, except one place on Long Island, and that was all raked up long ago. All the rest about him is just silly nonsense and talk. He never *was* much of a pirate, anyway!"

"Yes, I discovered the same thing in the book I had about him," agreed Doris. "We'll have to give up Captain Kidd, but there were some pirates who did bury somewhere, and one I discovered about did a lot of work right around these shores."

"He *did*?" cried Sally, almost losing her oars in her excitement. "Who was he? Tell me—quick!"

"His name was Richard Worley," answered Doris. "He was a pirate about the year 1718, the same time that Blackbeard and Stede Bonnet were 'pirating' too."

"Yes, I know about them," commented Sally. "I read of them in that book. But it didn't say anything about Worley."

"Well, he was only a pirate for six weeks before he was captured," went on Doris, "but in that time he managed to do a lot, and it was all along the coast of New Jersey here. Now why isn't it quite possible that he sailed in here with his loot and made that nice little cave and buried his treasure, intending to come back some time. He was captured finally down off the coast of the Carolinas, but he might easily have disposed of his booty here before that."

Sally was filled with elated certainty. "It surely must have been he!" she cried. "For there was some one,—that's certain, or there wouldn't have been so much talk about buried treasure. And he's the likeliest person to have made that cave."

"There's just one drawback that I can see," Doris reminded her. "It was an awfully long time ago,—1718, nearly two hundred years. Do you think it would all have lasted so long? The wood and all, I mean?"

"That cedar wood lasts forever," declared Sally. "He probably wrecked some vessel and then took the wood and built this cave with it. Probably he built it because he thought it would be a good place to hide in some time, if they got to chasing him. No one in all the world would ever find him there."

"That's a good idea!" commented Doris. "I'd been wondering why a pirate should take such trouble to fix up a place like that. They usually just dug a hole and put in the treasure and then killed one of their own number and buried his body on top of it. I hope to goodness that Mr. Richard Worley didn't do that pleasant little trick! When we find the treasure, we don't want any skeletons mixed up with it."

They both laughed heartily over the conceit, and rowed with increased vigor as Slipper Point came in sight.

"You said you had an idea about that queer paper we found, too," Sally reminded her. "What was it?"

"Oh, I don't know whether it amounts to much, and I'll try to explain it later. The first thing to do is to try to discover, if we can, some idea of a date, or something connected with this cave, so that we can see if we are on the right track. I've been thinking that if that wood was from an old, wrecked vessel, we might perhaps find something on it somewhere that would give us a clue."

"That's so," said Sally. "I hadn't thought of that before."

With this in mind, they entered the cave, lit the candle, seated Genevieve on the chair with a bag of candy in her lap for solace, and proceeded to their task.

"The only way to find anything is just to scrape off all we can of this mold," announced Sally. "You take one side, and I'll take the other and we'll use these sticks. It won't be an easy job."

It was not. For over an hour they both dug away, scraping off what they could of the moss and fungus that covered the cedar planks. Doris made so little progress that she finally procured the ancient knife from the table and worked more easily with that implement. Not a vestige nor a trace of any writing was visible anywhere.

When the arms of both girls had begun to ache cruelly, and Genevieve had grown restless and was demanding to "go out," Sally suggested that they give it up for the day. But just at that moment, working in a far corner, Doris had stumbled upon a clue. The rusty knife had struck a curious knobby break in the wood, which, on further scraping, developed the shape of a raised letter "T." At her exultant cry, Sally rushed over and frantically assisted in the quest. Scraping and digging for another fifteen minutes revealed at last a name, raised on the thick planking, which had evidently been the stern name-plate of the vessel. When it all stood revealed, the writing ran:

The Anne Arundel
England 1843.

The two stood gazing at it a moment in puzzled silence. Then Doris threw down her knife.

"It's all off with the pirate theory, Sally!" she exclaimed.

"Why so?" demanded her companion, mystified for the moment.

"Just because," answered Doris, "if Richard Worley lived in 1718, he couldn't possibly have built a cave with the remains of a vessel dated 1843, and neither could any other pirate, for there weren't any more pirates as late as 1843. Don't you see?"

Sally did see and her countenance fell.

"Then what in the world *is* the mystery?" she cried.

"That we've got to find the answer to in some other way," replied Doris, "for we're as much in the dark as ever!"

CHAPTER VII

THE FIRST CLUE

IT was a discouraged pair that rowed home from Slipper Point that morning. Sally was depressed beyond words by their recent discovery, for she had counted many long months on her "pirate theory" and the ultimate unearthing of buried treasure. Doris, however, was not so much depressed as she was baffled by this curious turn of the morning's investigation. Thinking hard, she suddenly shipped her oars and turned about to face Sally with an exultant little exclamation.

"Do you realize that we've made a very valuable find this morning, after all, Sally?" she cried.

"Why, no, I don't. Everything's just spoiled!" retorted Sally dubiously. "If it isn't pirates, it isn't anything that's *worth* anything, is it?"

"I don't know yet how much it's worth," retorted Doris, "but I do know that we've unearthed enough to start us on a new hunt."

"Well, what is it?" demanded Sally, still incredulous.

"Can't you guess? The *name* of this vessel that the lumber came from,—and the *date*. Whatever happened that cave couldn't have been made before 1843, anyhow, and that isn't so terribly long ago. There might even be persons alive here today who could remember as far back as that date, if not further. And if this *Anne Arundel* was wrecked somewhere about here, perhaps there's some one who will remember that, and—"

But here Sally interrupted her with an excited cry. "My grandfather!—He surely would know. He was born in 1830, 'cause he's eighty-seven now, and he ought to remember if there was a wreck on this beach when he was thirteen years old or older. He remembers lots about wrecks. I'll ask him."

Doris recalled the hearty old sea-captain, Sally's grandfather, whom she had often seen sitting on Sally's own front porch, or down at the Landing. That he could remember many tales of wrecks and storms she did not doubt, and her spirits rose with Sally's.

"But you must go about it carefully," she warned. "Don't let him know, at first that you know much about the *Anne Arundel*, or he'll begin to suspect something and ask questions. I don't see quite how you *are* going to find out about it without asking him anyway."

"You leave that to me!" declared Sally. "Grandfather's great on spinning yarns when he gets going. And he grows so interested about it generally that he doesn't realize afterward whether he's told you a thing or you've asked him about it, 'cause he has so much to tell and gets so excited about it. Oh, I'll find out about the *Anne Arundel*, all right—if there's anything *to* find out!"

They parted that morning filled anew with the spirit of adventure and mystery, stopping no longer to consider the dashed hopes of the earlier day.

"I probably shan't get a chance to talk to Grandfather alone before evening," said Sally in parting, "though I'm going to be around most of the afternoon where he is. But I'll surely talk to him tonight when he's smoking on our porch and Mother and Dad are away at the Landing. Then I'll find out what he knows, and let you know tomorrow morning."

It was a breathless and excited Sally that rowed up to the hotel at an early hour next day.

"Did he say anything?" demanded Doris breathlessly, flying down to the sand to meet her.

"Come out in the boat," answered Sally, "and I'll tell you all about it. He certainly *did* say something!"

Doris clambered into the boat, and they headed as usual for Slipper Point.

"Well?" queried Doris, impatiently, when they were in midstream.

"Grandfather was good and ready to talk wrecks with me last night," began Sally, "for there was no one else about to talk to. You know, the pavilion opened for dancing the first time this season, and every one made a bee-line for that. Grandfather never goes down to the Landing at night, so he was left stranded for some one to talk to and was right glad to have me. I began by asking him to tell me something about when he was a young man and how things were around here and how he came to go to sea. It always pleases him to pieces to be asked to tell about those times, so he sailed in and I didn't do a thing but sit and listen, though I've heard most of all that before.

"But after a while he got to talking about how he'd been shipwrecked and along about there I saw how it would be easy to switch him off to the shipwrecks that happened around here. When I did that he had plenty to tell me and it was rather interesting too. By and by I said, just quietly, as if I wasn't awfully interested:

" 'Grandfather, I've heard tell of a ship called the *Anne Arundel* that was wrecked about here once. Do you know anything of her?' And he said he just guessed he *did*. She came ashore one winter night, along about 1850, in the worst storm they'd ever had on this coast. He was a young man of twenty then and he helped to rescue some of the sailors and passengers. She was a five-masted schooner, an English ship, and she just drove right up on the shore and went to pieces. They didn't get many of her crew off alive, as most of them had been swept overboard in the heavy seas.

"But, listen to this. He said that the queer part of it all was that, though her hulk and wreckage lay on the beach for a couple of months or so, and nobody gave it any attention, suddenly, in one week, it all disappeared as clean as if another hurricane had hit it and carried it off. But this wasn't the case, because there had been fine weather for a long stretch. Everybody wondered and wondered what had become of the *Anne Arundel* but nobody ever found out. It seemed particularly strange because no one, not even beach-combers, would be likely to carry off a whole wreck, bodily, like that."

"And he never had a suspicion," cried Doris, "that some one had taken it to build that little cave up the river? How perfectly wonderful, Sally!"

"No, but there's something about it that puzzles me a lot," replied Sally. "They took it to fix up that cave, sure enough. But, do you realize, Doris, that it only took a small part of a big vessel like that, to build the cave. What became of all the rest of it? Why was it all taken, when so little of it was needed? What was it used for?"

This was as much a puzzle to Doris as to Sally. "I'm sure I can't imagine," she replied. "But one thing's certain. We've got to find out who took it and why, if it takes all summer. By the way! I've got a new idea about why that cave was built. I believe it was for some one who wanted to hide away,—a prisoner escaped from jail, for instance, or some one who was afraid of being put in prison because he'd done something wrong, or it was thought that he had. How about that?"

"Then what about the queer piece of writing we found?" demanded Sally. Doris had to admit she could not see where that entered into things.

"Well," declared Sally, at length, "I've got a brand new idea about it too. It came from something else Grandfather was telling me last night. If it wasn't pirates it was—*smugglers*!"

"Mercy!" cried Doris. "What makes you think so?"

"Because Grandfather was telling me of a lot of smugglers who worked a little farther down the coast. They used to run in to one of the rivers with a small schooner they cruised in, and hide lots of stuff that they'd have to pay duty on if they brought it in the proper way. They hid it in an old deserted house near the shore and after a while would sell what they had and bring in some more. By and by the government officers got after them and caught them all.

"It just set me to thinking that this might be another hiding place that was never discovered, and this bit of paper the secret plan to show where or how they hid the stuff. Perhaps they were all captured at some time, and never got back here to find the rest of their things. I tell you, we may find some treasure yet, though it probably won't be like what the pirates would have hidden."

Doris was decidedly fired by the new idea. "It sounds quite possible to me," she acknowledged, "and what we want to do now is to try and work out the meaning of that queer bit of paper."

"Yes, and by the way, you said quite a while ago that you had an idea about that," Sally reminded her. "What was it?"

"Oh, I don't know as it amounts to much," said Doris. "So many things have happened since, that I've half forgotten about it. But if we're going up to Slipper Point, I can show you better when we get there. Do you know, Sally, I believe I'm just as much interested if that's a smuggler's cave as if it had been a pirate's. It's actually thrilling!"

And without further words, they bent their energies toward reaching their destination.

CHAPTER VIII

ROUNDTREE'S

AT Slipper Point, they established Genevieve, as usual, on the old chair in the cave, to examine by candle-light the new picture-book that Doris had brought for her. This was calculated to keep her quiet for a long while, as she was inordinately fond of "picters," as she called them.

"Now," cried Sally, "what about that paper?"

"Oh, I don't know that it amounts to very much," explained Doris. "It just occurred to me, in looking it over, that possibly the fact of its being square and the little cave also being square might have something to do with things. Suppose the floor of the cave were divided into squares just as this paper is. Now do you notice one thing? Read the letters in their order up from the extreme left hand corner diagonally. It reads r-i-g-h-t-s and the last square is blank. Now why couldn't that mean 'right' and the 's' stand for square,—the 'right square' being that blank one in the extreme corner?"

"Goody!" cried Sally. "That's awfully clever of you. I never thought of such a thing as reading it that way, in all the time I had it. And do you think that perhaps the treasure is buried under there?"

"Well, of course, that's all we *can* think it means. It might be well to investigate in that corner."

But another thought had occurred to Sally. "If that's so," she inquired dubiously, "what's the use of all the rest of those letters and numbers. They must be there for *something*."

"They may be just a 'blind,' and mean nothing at all," answered Doris. "You see they'd have to fill up the spaces somehow, or else, if I'm right, they'd have more than one vacant square. And one was all they wanted. So they filled up the rest with a lot of letters and figures just to puzzle any one that got hold of it. But there's something else I've thought of about it. You notice that the two outside lines of squares that lead up to the empty squares are just numbers,—not letters at all. Now I've added each line together and find that the sum of each side is exactly *twenty-one*. Why wouldn't it be possible that it means the sides of this empty square are twenty-one—something—in length. It can't possibly mean twenty-one *feet* because the whole cave is only about nine feet square. It must mean twenty-one inches."

Sally was quite overcome with amazement at this elaborate system of reasoning it out. "You certainly are a wonder!" she exclaimed. "I never would have thought of it in the world."

"Why, it was simple," declared Doris, "for just as soon as I'd hit upon that first idea, the rest all followed like clockwork. But now, if all this is right, and the treasure lies somewhere under the vacant square, our business is to find it."

Suddenly an awful thought occurred to Sally. "But how are you going to know *which* corner that square is in? It might be any of the four, mightn't it?"

For a moment Doris was stumped. How, indeed, were they going to tell? Then one solution dawned on her. "Wouldn't they have been most likely to consider the square of the floor as it faces you, coming in at the door, to be the way that corresponds to the plan on the paper? In that case, the extreme right-hand corner from the door, for the space of twenty-one inches, is the spot."

It certainly seemed the most logical conclusion. They rushed over to the spot and examined it, robbing Genevieve of her candle in order to have the most light on the dark corner. It exhibited, however, no signs of anything the least unusual about it. The rough planks of the flooring joined quite closely to those of the wall, and there was no evidence of its having ever been used as a place of concealment. At this discouraging revelation, their faces fell.

"Let's examine the other corners," suggested Doris. "Perhaps we're not right about this being the one."

The others, however, revealed no difference in their appearance, and the girls restored her candle to Genevieve at the table, and stood gazing at each other in disconcerted silence.

"But, after all," suggested Doris shortly, "would you expect to see any real sign of the boards being movable or having been moved at some time? That would only give their secret away, when you come to think of it. No, if there *is* some way of opening one of those corners, it's pretty carefully concealed, and I don't see anything for it but for us to bring some tools up here,—a hammer and saw and chisel, perhaps,—and go to work prying those boards up." The plan appealed to Sally.

"I'll get some of Dad's," she declared. "He's got a lot of tools in the boathouse, and he'd never miss a few of the older ones. We'll bring them up tomorrow and begin. And I think your first idea about the corner was the best. We'll start over there."

"I's cold," Genevieve began to whimper, at this point. "I don't *like* it in here. I want to go out."

The two girls laughed. "She isn't much of a treasure-hunter, is she!" said Doris. "Bless her heart. We'll go out right away and sit down under the pine trees."

They emerged into the sunlight, and Sally carefully closed and concealed the entrance to their secret lair. After the chill of the underground, the warm sunlight was very welcome and they lay lazily basking in its heat and inhaling the odor of the pine-needles. Far above their heads the fish-hawks swooped with their high-pitched piping cry, and two wrens scolded each other in the branches above their heads. Sally sat tailor-fashion, her chin cupped in her two hands, thinking in silence, while Doris, propped against a tree, was explaining the pictures in her new book to Genevieve. In the intervals, while Genevieve stared absorbedly at one of them, Doris would look about her curiously and speculatively. Suddenly she thrust the book aside and sprang to her feet.

"Do you realize, Sally," she exclaimed, "that I've never yet explored a bit of this region *above ground* with you? I've never seen a thing except this bit right about the cave. Why not take me all round here for a way. It might be quite interesting."

Sally looked both surprised and scornful. "There's nothing at all to see around here that's a bit interesting," she declared. "There's just this pine grove and the underbrush, and back there,—quite a way back, is an old country road. It isn't even worth getting all hot and tired going to see."

"Well, I don't care, I want to see it!" insisted Doris. "I somehow have a feeling that it would be worth while. And if you are too tired to come with me, I'll go by myself. You and Genevieve can rest here."

"No, I want to go wis Dowis!" declared Genevieve, scrambling to her feet as she scented a new diversion.

"Well, I'll go too," laughed Sally. "I'm not as lazy as all that, but I warn you, you won't find anything worth the trouble."

They set off together, scrambling through the scrub-oak and bay-bushes, stopping now and then to pick and devour wild strawberries, or gather a great handful of sassafras to chew. All the while Doris gazed about her curiously, asking every now and then a seemingly irrelevant question of Sally.

Presently they emerged from the pine woods and crossed a field covered only with wild blackberry vines still bearing their white blossoms. At the farther edge of this field they came upon a sandy road. It wound away in a hot ribbon till a turn hid it from sight, and the heat of the morning tempted them no further to explore it.

"This is the road I told you of," explained Sally with an "I-told-you-so" expression. "You see it isn't anything at all, only an old back road leading to Manituck. Nobody much comes this way if they can help it,—it's so sandy."

"But what's that old house there?" demanded Doris, pointing to an ancient, tumbledown structure not far away. "And isn't it the queerest-looking place, one part so gone to pieces and unkempt, and that other little wing all nicely fixed up and neat and comfortable!"

It was indeed an odd combination. The structure was a large old-fashioned farmhouse, evidently of a period dating well back in the nineteenth century. The main part had fallen into disuse, as was quite evident from the closed and shuttered windows, the peeling, blistered paint, the unkempt air of being not inhabited. But a tiny "L" at one side bore an aspect as different from the main building as could well be imagined. It had lately received a coat of fresh white paint. Its windows were wide open and daintily curtained with some pretty but inexpensive material. The little patch of flower-garden in front was as trim and orderly.

"I don't understand it," went on Doris. "What place is it?"

"Oh, that's only Roundtree's," answered Sally indifferently. "That's old Miss Roundtree now, coming from the back. She lives there all alone."

As she was speaking, the person in question came into view from around the back of the house, a basket of vegetables in her hand. Plainly she had just been picking them in the vegetable-garden, a portion of which was visible at the side of the house. She sat down presently on her tiny front porch, removed her large sun-bonnet and began to sort them over. From their vantage-point behind some tall bushes at the roadside, the girls could watch her unobserved.

"I like her looks," whispered Doris after a moment. "Who is she and why does she live in this queer little place?"

"I told you her name was Roundtree,—Miss Camilla Roundtree," replied Sally. "Most folks call her 'old Miss Camilla' around here. She's awfully poor, though they say her folks were quite rich at one time, and she's quite deaf too. That big old place was her father's, and I s'pose is hers now, but she can't afford to keep it up, she has so little money. So she just lives in that small part, and she knits for a living,—caps and sweaters and things like that. She does knit beautifully and gets quite a good many orders, especially in summer, but even so it hardly brings her in enough to live on. She's kind of queer too, folks think. But I don't see why you're so interested in her."

"I like her looks," answered Doris. "She has a fine face. Somehow she seems to me like a lady,—a *real* lady!"

"Well, she sort of puts on airs, folks think, and she doesn't care to associate with everybody," admitted Sally. "But she's awfully good and kind, too. Goes and nurses people when they're sick or have any trouble, and never charges for it, and all that sort of thing. But, same time, she always seems to want to be by herself. She reads lots, too, and has no end of old books. They say they were her father's. Once she lent me one or two when I went to get her to make a sweater for Genevieve."

"Oh, do you know her?" cried Doris. "How interesting!"

"Why, yes, of course I know her. Everyone does around here. But I don't see anything very interesting about it." To tell the truth, Sally was quite puzzled by Doris's absorption in the subject. It was Genevieve who broke the spell.

"I's sirsty!" she moaned. "I want a djink. I want Mis Camilla to gi' me a djink!"

"Come on!" cried Doris to Sally. "If you know her, we can easily go over and ask her for a drink. I'm crazy to meet her."

Still wondering, Sally led the way over to the tiny garden and the three proceeded up the path toward Miss Roundtree.

"Why, good morning!" exclaimed that lady, looking up. Her voice was very soft, and a little toneless, as is often the case with the deaf.

"Good morning!" answered Sally in a rather loud tone, and a trifle awkwardly presented Doris. But there was no awkwardness in the manner with which Miss Camilla acknowledged the new acquaintance. Indeed it was suggestive of an old-time courtesy, now growing somewhat obsolete. And Doris had a chance to gaze, at closer range, on the fine, high-bred face framed in its neatly parted gray hair.

"Might Genevieve have a drink?" asked Doris at length. "She seems to be very thirsty."

"Why, assuredly!" exclaimed Miss Camilla. "Come inside, all of you, and rest in the shade." So they trooped indoors, into Miss Camilla's tiny sitting-room, while she herself disappeared into the still tinier kitchen at the back. While she was gone, Doris gazed about with a new wonder and admiration in her eyes.

The room was speckless in its cleanliness, and full of many obviously home-made contrivances and makeshifts. Yet there were two or three beautiful pieces of old mahogany furniture, of a satiny finish and ancient date. And on the mantel stood one marvelous little piece of pottery that, even to Doris's untrained eye, gave evidence of being a rare and costly bit. But Miss Camilla was now coming back, bearing a tray on which stood three glasses of water and a plate of cookies and three little dishes of delicious strawberries.

"You children must be hungry after your long morning's excursion," she said. "Try these strawberries of mine. They have just come from the garden."

Doris thought she had never tasted anything more delightful than that impromptu little repast. And when it was over, she asked Miss Camilla a question, for she had been chatting with her all along, in decided contrast to the rather embarrassed silence of Sally.

"What is that beautiful little vase you have there, Miss Roundtree, may I ask? I've been admiring it a lot." A wonderful light shone suddenly in Miss Camilla's eyes. Here, it was plain, was her hobby.

"That's a Louis XV Sèvres," she explained, patting it lovingly. "It *is* marvelous, isn't it, and all I have left of a very pretty collection. It was my passion once, this pottery, and I had the means to indulge it. But they are all gone now, all but this one. I shall never part with this." The light died out of her eyes as she placed the precious piece back on the mantel.

"Good-bye. Come again!" she called after them, as they took their departure. "I always enjoy talking to you children."

When they had retraced their way to the boat and pushed off and were making all speed for the hotel, Sally suddenly turned to Doris and demanded:

"Why in the world are you so interested in Miss Camilla? I've known her all my life, and I never talked so much to her in all that time as you did this morning."

"Well, to begin with," replied Doris, shipping her oars and facing her friend for a moment, "I think she's a lovely and interesting person. But there's something else besides." She stopped abruptly, and Sally, filled with curiosity, demanded impatiently,

"Well?"

Doris's reply almost caused her to lose her oars in her astonishment.

"I think she knows all about that cave!"

CHAPTER IX

DORIS HAS A NEW THEORY

"WELL, for gracious sake!" was all Sally could reply to this astonishing remark. And a moment later, "How on earth do you know?"

"I don't *know*. I'm only guessing at it," replied Doris. "But I have one or two good reasons for thinking we've been on the wrong track right along. And if I'd known about *her* before, I'd have thought so long ago."

"But what *is* it?" cried Sally again, bursting with impatience and curiosity.

"Sally," said Doris soberly, "I'm going to ask you not to make me explain it all just yet. I would if I had it all clear in my mind, but the whole idea is just as hazy as can be at present. And you know a thing is very hard to explain when it's hazy like that. It sounds silly if you put it into words. So won't you just let it be till I get it better thought out?"

"Why, yes, of course," replied Sally with an assumed heartiness that she was far from feeling. Truth to tell, she was not only badly disappointed but filled with an almost uncontrollable curiosity to know what Doris had discovered about her secret that she herself did not know.

"And I'm going to ask you another thing," went on Doris. "Do you suppose any one around here knows much about the history of Miss Camilla and her family? Would your grandfather be likely to know?"

"Why, yes, I guess so," replied Sally. "If anybody knows I'm sure it would be he, because he's the oldest person around here."

"Then," said Doris, "I want you to let me talk to your grandfather about it. We'll both seem to be talking to him together, but I want to ask him some questions very specially myself. But I don't want him to suspect that we have any special interest in the thing, so you try and make him talk the way you did that night when he told you all about the wrecks, and the *Anne Arundel*. Will you?"

"Oh, yes," agreed Sally. "That's easy. When shall we do it? This afternoon? I think he'll be down at the Landing, and we won't have any trouble getting him to talk to us. There aren't many around the Landing yet, 'cause the season is so early, and I'll steer him over into a corner where we can be by ourselves."

"That's fine!" cried Doris. "I knew you could manage it."

"But tell me—just one thing," begged Sally, "What made you first think that Miss Camilla had anything to do with this? You can tell me just *that*, can't you?"

"It was the little Sèvres vase on the mantel," explained Doris, "and the way she spoke of it, I know a little,—just a tiny bit about old china and porcelains, because my grandfather is awfully interested in them and has collected quite a lot. But it was the way she *spoke* of it that made me think."

Not another word would she say on the subject. And though Sally racked her brains over the matter for the rest of the day, she could find no point where Miss Camilla and her remarks had the slightest bearing on that secret of theirs.

It was about two o'clock that afternoon, and the pavilion at the Landing was almost deserted. Later it would be peopled by a throng, young and old, hiring boats, crabbing from the long dock, drinking soda-water or merely watching the river life, idly. But, during the two or three hot hours directly after noon, it was deserted. On this occasion, however, not for long. Old Captain Carter, corn-cob pipe in mouth, and stumping loudly on his wooden leg, was approaching down the road from the village. At this hour he seldom failed to take his seat in a corner of the pavilion and wait patiently for the afternoon crowd to appear. His main diversion for the day consisted in his chats with the throngs who haunted the Landing.

He had not been settled in his corner three minutes, his wooden leg propped on another chair, when up the wide stairs from the beach appeared his two granddaughters, accompanied by another girl. Truth to tell, they had been waiting below exactly half an hour for this very event. Doris, who had met him before, went over and exchanged the greetings of the day, then casually settled herself in an adjacent chair, fanning herself frantically and exclaiming over the heat. Sally and Genevieve next strolled up and perched on a bench close by. For several minutes the two girls exchanged some rather desultory conversation. Then, what appeared to be a chance remark of Doris's but was in reality carefully planned, drew the old sea-captain into their talk.

"I wonder why some people around here keep a part of their houses nicely fixed and live in that part and let the rest get all run down and go to waste?" she inquired with elaborate indifference. Captain Carter pricked up his ears.

"*Who* do that, I'd like to know?" he snorted. "I hain't seen many of 'em!"

"Well, I passed a place this morning and it looked that way," Doris went on. "I thought maybe it was customary in these parts."

"Where was it?" demanded the Captain, on the defensive for his native region.

"Way up the river," she answered, indicating the direction of Slipper Point.

"Oh, *that*!" he exclaimed in patent relief. "That's only Miss Roundtree's, and I guess you won't see another like it in a month of Sundays."

"Who is she and why does she do it?" asked Doris with a great (and this time real) show of interest. And thus, finding what his soul delighted in, a willing and interested listener, Captain Carter launched into a history and description of Miss Camilla Roundtree. He had told all that Sally had already imparted, when Doris broke in with some skilfully directed questions.

"How do you suppose she lost all her money?"

"Blest if I know, or any one else!" he grunted. "And what's more, I don't believe *she* lost it all, either. I think it was her father and her brother before her that did the trick. They were great folks around here,—high and mighty, we called 'em. Nobody among us down at the village was good enough for 'em. This here Miss Camilla,—her mother died when she was a baby—she used to spend most of her time in New York with a wealthy aunt. Some swell, she was!—used to go with her aunt pretty nigh every year to Europe and we didn't set eyes on her once in a blue moon. Her father and brother had a fine farm and were making money, but she didn't care for this here life.

"Well, one time she come back from Europe and things didn't seem to be going right down here at her place. I don't know what it was, but there were queer things whispered about the two men folks and all the money seemed to be gone suddenly, too. I was away at the time on a three-years' cruise, so I didn't hear nothin' about it till long after. But they say the brother he disappeared and never came back, and the father died suddenly of apoplexy or something, and Miss Camilla was left to shift for herself, on a farm mortgaged pretty nigh up to the hilt.

"She was a bright woman as ever was made, though, I'll say that for her, and she kept her head in the air and took to teaching school. She taught right good, too, for a number of years and got the mortgages off the farm. And then, all of a sudden, she began to get deaf-like, and couldn't go on teaching. Then she took to selling off a lot of their land lying round, and got through somehow on that, for a while. But times got harder and living higher priced, and finally she had to give up trying to keep the whole thing decent and just scrooged herself into those little quarters in the 'L.' She's made a good fight, but she never would come down off her high horse or ask for any help or let any one into what happened to her folks."

"How long ago was all that?" asked Doris.

"Oh, about forty or fifty years, I should think," he replied, after a moment's thought. "Yes, fifty or more, at the least."

"You say they owned a lot of land around their farm?" interrogated Doris, casually.

"Surest thing! One time old Caleb Roundtree owned pretty nigh the whole side of the river up that way, but he'd sold off a lot of it himself before he died. She owned a good patch for a while, though, several hundred acres, I guess. But she hain't got nothin' but what lies right around the house, now."

"Didn't you ever hear what happened to the brother?" demanded Doris.

"Never a thing. He dropped out of life here as neatly and completely as if he'd suddenly been dropped into the sea. And by the time I'd got back from my voyage the nine-days' wonder about it all was over, and I never could find out any more on the subject. Never was particularly interested to, either. Miss Camilla hain't nothin' to me. She's always kept to herself and so most folks have almost forgotten who she is."

As the Captain had evidently reached the end of his information on the subject, Doris rose to take her leave and Sally followed her eagerly.

"Well, did you find out what you wanted?" she cried, as soon as they were once more out on the river in old "45."

"I found out enough," answered Doris very seriously, "to make me feel pretty sure I'm right. Of course, I can only guess at lots of it, but *one* thing I'm certain of: that cave had nothing to do with smugglers or pirates—or anything of that sort!"

Sally dropped her oars with a smothered cry of utmost disappointment.

"I can't believe it!" she cried. "I just can't. I've counted on it *so* long—finding treasure or something like that, I mean. I just can't believe it isn't so."

"It may be something far more interesting," Doris replied soothingly. "But there's just one trouble about it. If it's what I think it is, and concerns Miss Camilla, I've begun to feel that we haven't any business meddling with it now. We oughtn't even to go into it."

Sally uttered a moan of absolute despair. "I thought it would be that way," she muttered, half to herself, "if I shared the secret. I *knew* they'd take it away from me!" She shipped her oars and buried her face in her hands. After a moment she raised her head defiantly. "Why, I don't even know why you say so. You haven't told me yet a single thing of what it's all about. Why *should* I stay away from that place?"

"Listen, Sally," said Doris, also shipping her oars and laying an appealing hand on her arm, "I ought to tell you now, and I will. Perhaps you won't feel the same about it as I do. We can talk that over afterward. But don't feel so badly about it. Just hear what I have to say first.

"I think there has been some trouble in Miss Camilla's life,—something she couldn't tell any one about, and probably connected with that cave. What your grandfather said about her father and brother makes me all the more sure of it. I believe one or the other of them did something wrong,—something connected with money, perhaps, embezzled it or forged checks or something of that kind. And perhaps whoever it was had to hide away and be kept so for a long time, and so that cave was made and he hid there. Don't you remember, your grandfather said the brother disappeared suddenly and never came back? It must have been he, then. And perhaps Miss Camilla had to sell most of her valuable things and make up what he had done. That would explain her having parted with all her lovely porcelains and china. And if so much of the land around the house once belonged to her, probably that part where the cave is did too."

"But what about that bit of paper, then?" demanded Sally, who had been drinking in this explanation eagerly. "I don't see what that would have to do with it."

"Well, I don't either," confessed Doris. "Perhaps it *is* the plan of the place where something is hidden, but I'm somehow beginning to think it isn't. I'll have to think that over later.

"But now, can't you see that if what I've said is right, it wouldn't be the thing for us to do any more prying into poor Miss Camilla's secret? It would really be a dreadful thing, especially if she ever suspected that we knew. She probably doesn't dream that another soul in the world knows of it at all."

Sally was decidedly impressed with this explanation and argument, but she had one more plea to put forward.

"What you say sounds very true, Doris, and I've almost got to believe it, whether I want to or not. But I'm going to ask just one thing. Let's give our other idea just a trial, anyway. Let's go there once more and see if that scheme about the floor and the place in the corner is any good. It *might* be, you know. It sounded awfully good to me. And it won't hurt a thing for us to try it out. If we don't find anything, we'll know there's nothing in it. And if we do find anything that concerns Miss Camilla, we'll let it alone and never go near the place again. What do you say?"

Doris thought it over gravely. The argument seemed quite sound, and yet some delicate instinct in her still urged that they should meddle no further. But, after all, she considered, they were sure of nothing. It might have no concern with Miss Camilla at all. And, to crown it, the secret was Sally's originally, when all was said and done. Who was she, Doris, to dictate what should or should not be done about it? She capitulated.

"All right, Sally," she agreed. "I believe it can do no harm to try out our original scheme. We'll get at it first thing tomorrow morning."

CHAPTER X

BEHIND THE CEDAR PLANK

THEY set out on the following morning. Elaborate preparations had been made for the undertaking and, so that they might have ample time undisturbed, Doris had begged her mother to allow her to picnic for the day with Sally, and not come back to the hotel for luncheon. As Mrs. Craig had come to have quite a high opinion of Sally, her judgment and knowledge of the river and vicinity, she felt no hesitation in trusting Doris to be safe with her.

Sally had provided the sandwiches and Doris was armed with fruit and candy and books to amuse Genevieve. In the bow of the boat Sally had stowed away a number of tools borrowed from her father's boathouse. Altogether, the two girls felt as excited and mysterious and adventurous as could well be imagined.

"I wish we could have left Genevieve at home," whispered Sally as they were embarking. "But there's no one to take care of her for all day, so of course it was impossible. But I'm afraid she's going to get awfully tired and restless while we're working."

"Oh, never you fear!" Doris encouraged her. "I've brought a few new picture-books and we'll manage to keep her amused somehow."

Once established in the cave, having settled Genevieve with a book, the girls set to work in earnest.

"I'm glad I thought to bring a dozen more candles," said Sally. "We were down to the end of the last one. Now shall we begin on that corner at the extreme right-hand away from the door? That's the likeliest place. I'll measure a space around it twenty-one inches square."

She measured off the space on the floor carefully with a folding ruler, while Doris stood over her watching with critical eyes. Then, having drawn the lines with a piece of chalk, Sally proceeded to begin on the sawing operation with one of her father's old and somewhat rusty saws.

It was a heartbreakingly slow operation. Turn and turn about they worked away, encouraging each other with cheering remarks. The planks of the old *Anne Arundel* were very thick and astonishingly tough. At the end of an hour they had but one side of the square sawed through, and Genevieve was beginning to grow fractious. Then they planned it that while one worked, the other should amuse the youngest member of the party by talking, singing, and showing pictures to her.

This worked well for a time, and a second side at last was completed. By the time they reached the third, however, Genevieve flatly refused to remain in the cave another moment, so it was agreed that one of them should take her outside while the other remained within and sawed. This proved by far the best solution yet, as Genevieve very shortly fell asleep on the warm pine needles. They covered her with a shawl they had brought, and then both went back to the undertaking, of which they were now, unconfessedly, very weary.

It was shortly after the noon hour when the saw made its way through the fourth side of the square. In a hush of breathless expectation, they lifted the piece of timber, prepared for—who could tell what wondrous secret beneath it?

The space it left was absolutely empty of the slightest suggestion of anything remarkable. It revealed the sandy soil of the embankment into which the cave was dug, and nothing else whatever. The disgusted silence that followed Doris was the first to break.

"Of course, something may be buried down here, but I doubt it awfully. I'm sure we would have seen some sign of it, if this had been the right corner. However, give me that trowel, Sally, and we'll dig down a way." She dug for almost a foot into the damp sand, and finally gave it up.

"How could any one go on digging down in the space of only twenty-one inches?" she exclaimed in despair. "If one were to dig at all, the space ought to be much larger. No, this very plainly isn't the right corner. Let's go outside and eat our lunch, and then, if we have any courage left, we can come back and begin on another corner. Personally, I feel as if I should scream, if I had to put my hand to that old saw again!"

But a hearty luncheon and a half hour of idling in the sunlight above ground after it, served to restore their courage and determination. Sally was positive that the corner diagonally opposite was the one most likely to yield results, and Doris was inclined to agree with her. Genevieve, however, flatly refused to re-enter the cave so they were forced to adopt the scheme of the morning, one remaining always outdoors with her, as they did not dare let her roam around by herself. Sally volunteered to take the first shift at the sawing, and after they had measured off the twenty-one inch square in the opposite corner she set to work, while Doris stayed outside with Genevieve.

Seated with a picture-book open on her lap, and with Genevieve cuddled close by her side, she was suddenly startled by a muffled, excited cry from within the cave. Obviously, something had happened. Springing up, she hurried inside, Genevieve trailing after her. She beheld Sally standing in the middle of the cave, candle in hand, dishevelled and excited, pointing to the side of the cave near which she had been working.

"Look, look!" she cried. "What did I tell you?" Doris looked, expecting to see something about the floor in the corner to verify their surmises. The sight that met her eyes was as different as possible from that.

A part of the wall of the cave, three feet in width and reaching from top to bottom had opened and swung inward like a door on its hinges.

"What *is* it?" she breathed in a tone of real awe.

"It's a *door*, just as it looks," explained Sally, "and we never even guessed it was there. I happened to be leaning against that part of the wall as I sawed, balancing myself against it, and sometimes pushing pretty hard. All of a sudden it gave way, and swung out like that, and I almost tumbled in. I was so astonished I hardly knew what had happened!"

"But what's behind it?" cried Doris, snatching the candle and hurrying forward to investigate. They peered together into the blackness back of the newly revealed door, the candle held high above their heads.

"Why, it's a *tunnel*!" exclaimed Sally. "A great, long tunnel, winding away. I can't even see how far it goes. Did you ever?"

The two girls stood looking at each other and at the opening in a maze of incredulous speculation. Suddenly Sally uttered a satisfied cry.

"I know! I know, now! We never could think where all the rest of the wood from the *Anne Arundel* went. It's right here!" It was evidently true. The tunnel had been lined, top and bottom and often at the sides with the same planking that had lined the cave and at intervals there were stout posts supporting the roof of it. Well and solidly had it been constructed in that long ago period, else it would never have remained intact so many years.

"Doris," said Sally presently, "where do you suppose this leads to?"

"I haven't the faintest idea," replied her friend, "except that it probably leads to the treasure or the secret, or whatever it is. That much I'm certain of now."

"So am I," agreed Sally, "but, here's the important thing. Are we to go in there and find it?"

Doris shrank back an instant. "Oh, I don't know!" she faltered. "I'm not sure whether I dare to—or whether Mother would allow me to—if she knew. It—it *might* be dangerous. Something might give way and bury us alive."

"Well, I'll tell you what I'll do," announced Sally courageously. "I'll take a candle and go in a way by myself and see what it's like. You stay here with Genevieve, and I'll keep calling back to you, so you needn't worry about me." Before Doris could argue the question with her, she had lighted another candle and stepped bravely into the gloom.

Doris, at the opening, watched her progress nervously, till a turn in the tunnel hid her from sight.

"Oh, Sally, do come back!" she called. "I can't stand this suspense!"

"I'm all right!" Sally shouted back. "After that turn it goes on straight for the longest way. I can't see the end. But it's perfectly safe. The planks are as strong as iron yet. There isn't a sign of a cave-in. I'm coming back a moment." She presently reappeared.

"Look here!" she demanded, facing her companion. "Are you game to come with me? We can bring Genevieve along. It's perfectly safe. If you're not, you can stay here with her and I'll go by myself. I'm determined to see the end of this." Her resolution fired Doris. After all, it could not be so very dangerous, since the tunnel seemed in such good repair. Forgetting all else in her enthusiasm, she hastily consented.

"We must take plenty of candles and matches," declared Sally. "We wouldn't want to be left in the dark in there. It's lucky I brought a lot today. Now, Genevieve, you behave yourself and come along like a good girl, and we'll buy you some lolly-pops when we get back home!" Genevieve was plainly reluctant to add her presence to the undertaking, but, neither, on the other hand, did she wish to be left behind, so she followed disapprovingly.

Each with a candle lit, they stepped down from the floor of the cave and gingerly progressed along the narrow way. Doris determinedly turned her eyes from the slugs and snails and strange insects that could be seen on the ancient planking, and kept them fastened on Sally's back as she led the way. On and on they went, silent, awe-stricken, and wondering. Genevieve whimpered and clung to Doris's skirts, but no one paid any attention to her, so she was forced to follow on, willy-nilly.

So far did this strange, underground passage proceed that Doris half-whispered: "Is it never going to end, Sally? Ought we to venture any further?"

"I'm going to the end!" announced Sally stubbornly. "You can go back if you like." And they all went on again in silence.

At length it was evident that the end was in sight, for the way was suddenly blocked by a stone wall, apparently, directly across the passage. They all drew a long breath and approached to examine it more closely. It was unmistakably a wall of stones, cemented like the foundation of a house, and beyond it they could not proceed.

"What are we going to do now?" demanded Doris.

"The treasure must be here," said Sally, "and I've found one thing that opened when you pushed against it. Maybe this is another. Let's try. Perhaps it's behind one of these stones. Look! The plaster seems to be loose around these in the middle." She thrust the weight of her strong young arm against it, directing it at the middle stone of three large ones, but without avail. They never moved the fraction of an inch. Then she began to push all along the sides where the plaster seemed loose. At last she threw her whole weight against it—and was rewarded!

The three stones swung round, as on a pivot, revealing a space only large enough to crawl through with considerable squeezing.

"Hurrah! hurrah!" she shouted. "What did I tell you, Doris? There's something else behind here,—another cave, I guess. I'm going through. Are you going to follow?" Handing her candle to Doris, she scrambled through the narrow opening. And Doris, now determined to stick at nothing, set both candles on the ground, and pushed the struggling and resisting Genevieve in next. After that, she passed in the candles to Sally, who held them while she clambered in herself.

And, once safely within, they stood and stared about them.

"Why, Sally," suddenly breathed Doris, "this isn't a cave. It's a *cellar*! Don't you see all the household things lying around? Garden tools, and vegetables and—and all that? Where in the world can we be?" A great light suddenly dawned on her.

"Sally Carter, what did I tell you? This cellar is Miss Camilla's. I know it. I'm *certain* of it. There's no other house anywhere near Slipper Point. I *told* you she knew about that cave!"

Sally listened, open-mouthed. "It can't be," she faltered. "I'm sure we didn't come in that direction at all."

"You can't tell how you're going—underground," retorted Doris. "Remember, the tunnel made a turn, too. Oh, Sally! Let's go back at once, before anything is discovered, and never, never let Miss Camilla or any one know what we've discovered. It's none of our business."

Sally, now convinced, was about to assent, when Genevieve suddenly broke into a loud howl.

"I won't go back! I won't go back—in that nas'y place!" she announced, at the top of her lungs.

"Oh, stop her!" whispered Doris. "Do stop

She led the others up the cellar steps

her, or Miss Camilla may hear!" Sally stifled her resisting sister by the simple process of placing her hand forcibly over her mouth,—but it was too late. A door opened at the top of a flight of steps, and Miss Camilla's astounded face appeared in the opening.

"What is it? Who is it?" she called, obviously frightened to death herself at this unprecedented intrusion. Huddled in a corner, they all shrank back for a moment, then Doris stepped boldly forward.

"It's only ourselves, Miss Camilla," she announced. "We have done a very dreadful thing, and we hadn't any right to do it. But, if you'll let us come upstairs, we'll explain it all, and beg your pardon, and promise never to speak of it or even think of it again." She led the others up the cellar steps, and into Miss Camilla's tiny, tidy kitchen. Here, still standing, she explained the whole situation to that lady, who was still too overcome with astonishment to utter a word. And she ended her explanation thus:

"So you see, we didn't have the slightest idea we were going to end at this house. But, all the same, we sort of felt that this cave was a secret of yours and that we really hadn't any right to be interfering with it. But won't you please forgive us, this time, Miss Camilla? And we'll really try to forget that it ever existed."

And then Miss Camilla suddenly found words. "My dear children," she stuttered, "I—I really don't know what you're talking about. I haven't the faintest idea what this all means. *I never knew till this minute that there was anything like a cave or a tunnel connected with this house!*"

And in the astounded silence that followed, the three stood gaping, open-mouthed, at each other.

CHAPTER XI

SOME BITS OF ROUNDTREE HISTORY

"BUT come into the sitting-room," at length commanded Miss Camilla, "and let us talk this strange thing over. You must be tired and hungry, too, after this awful adventure of coming through that dreadful tunnel. You must have some of this hot gingerbread and a glass of lemonade." And while she bustled about, on hospitable thoughts intent, they heard her muttering to herself:

"A cave—and a tunnel—and connected with *this* house!—What *can* it all mean?"

They sat in restful silence for a time, munching the delicious hot gingerbread and sipping cool lemonade. Never did a repast taste more welcome, coming as it did after the adventures and uncertainties of that eventful day. And while they ate, Miss Camilla sat wiping her glasses and putting them on and taking them off again and shaking her head over the perplexing news that had been so unexpectedly thrust upon her.

"I simply cannot understand it all," she began at last. "As I told you, I've never had the slightest idea of such a strange affair, nor can I imagine how it came there. When did you say that *Anne Arundel* vessel was wrecked?"

"Grandfather said in 1850," answered Sally.

"Eighteen hundred and fifty," mused Miss Camilla. "Well, I couldn't have been more than four or five years old, so of course I would scarcely remember it. Besides, I was not at home here a great deal. I used to spend most of my time with my aunt who lived in New York. She used to take me there for long visits, months on a stretch. If this cave and tunnel were made at that time, it was probably done while I was away, or else I would have known of it. My father and brother and one or two colored servants were the only ones in the house, most of the time. I had a nurse, an old Southern colored 'mammy' who always went about with me. She died about the time the Civil War broke out."

There was no light on the matter here. Miss Camilla relapsed again into puzzled silence, which the girls hesitated to intrude upon by so much as a single word, lest Miss Camilla should consider that they were prying into her past history.

"Wait a moment!" she suddenly exclaimed, sitting up very straight and wiping her glasses again in great excitement. "I believe I have the explanation." She looked about at her audience a minute, hesitantly. "I shall have to ask you girls please to keep what I am going to tell you entirely to yourselves. Few if any have ever known of it, and, though it would do no harm now, I have other reasons for not wishing it discussed publicly. Since you have discovered what you have, however, I feel it only right that you should know."

"You may rely on us, Miss Camilla," said Doris, speaking for them both, "to keep anything you may tell us a strict secret."

"Thank you," replied their hostess. "I feel sure of it. Well, I learned the fact, very early in my girlhood, that my father and also my brother, who was several years older than I, were both very strict and enthusiastic abolitionists. While slavery was still a national institution in this country, they were firm advocates of the freedom of the colored people. And, so earnest were they in the cause, that they became members of the great 'Underground Railway' system."

"What was that?" interrupted both girls at a breath.

"Did you never hear of it?" exclaimed Miss Camilla in surprise. "Why, it was a great secret system of assisting runaway slaves from the Southern States to escape from their bondage and get to Canada where they could no longer be considered any one's property. There were many people in all the Northern States, who, believing in freedom for the slaves, joined this secret league, and in their houses runaways would be sheltered, hidden and quietly passed on to the next house of refuge, or 'station,' as they were called, till at length the fugitives had passed the boundary of the country. It was, however, a severe legal offense to be caught assisting these fugitives, and the penalty was heavy fines and often imprisonment. But that did not daunt those whose hearts were in the cause. And so very secret was the whole organization that few were ever detected in it.

"It was in a rather singular way that I discovered my father to be concerned in this matter. I happened to be at home here, and came downstairs one morning, rather earlier than usual, to find our kitchen filled with a number of strange colored folk, in various stages of rags and hunger and evident excitement. I was a girl of ten or eleven at the time. Rushing to my father's study, I demanded an explanation of the strange spectacle. He took me aside and explained the situation to me, acknowledging that he was concerned in the 'Underground Railway' and warning me to maintain the utmost secrecy in the matter or it would imperil his safety.

"When I returned to the kitchen, to my astonishment, the whole crowd had mysteriously disappeared, though I had not been gone fifteen minutes. And I could not learn from any one a satisfactory explanation of their lightning disappearance. I should certainly have seen them, had they gone away above ground. I believe now that the cave and tunnel must have been the means of secreting them, and I haven't a doubt that my father and brother had had it constructed for that very purpose. A runaway, or even a number of them, could evidently be kept in the cave several days and then spirited away at night, probably by way of the river and some vessel out at sea that could take them straight to New York or even to Canada itself. Yes, it is all as clear as daylight to me now."

"But how do you suppose they were able to build the cave and tunnel and bring all the wood from the wreck on the beach without being discovered?" questioned Sally.

"That probably was not so difficult then as it would seem now," answered Miss Camilla. "To begin with, there were not so many people living about here then, and so there was less danger of being discovered. If my father and brother could manage to get men enough to help and a number of teams of oxen or horses such as he had, they could have brought the wreckage from the beach here, over what must then have been a very lonely and deserted road, without much danger of discovery. If it happened that at the time they were sheltering a number of escaped slaves, it would have been no difficult matter to press them into assisting on dark nights when they could be so well concealed. Yes, I think that was undoubtedly the situation."

They all sat quietly for a moment, thinking it over. Miss Camilla's solution of the cave and tunnel mystery was clear beyond all doubting, and it seemed as if there was nothing further for them to wonder about. Suddenly, however, Sally leaned forward eagerly.

"But did we tell you about the strange piece of paper we found under the old mattress, Miss Camilla? I've really forgotten what we did say."

Miss Camilla looked perplexed. "Why, no. I don't remember your mentioning it. Everything was so confused, at first, that I've forgotten it if you did. What about a piece of paper?"

"Here is a copy of what was on it," said Sally. "We never take the real piece away from where we first found it, but we made this copy. Perhaps you can tell what it all means." She handed the paper to Miss Camilla, who stared at it for several moments in blank bewilderment. Then she shook her head.

"I can't make anything of it at all," she acknowledged. "It must have been something left there by one of the fugitives. I don't believe it concerns me at all." She handed the paper back, but as she did so, a sudden idea occurred to Doris.

"Mightn't it have been some secret directions to the slaves left there for them by your father or brother?" she suggested. "Maybe it was to tell them where to go next, or something like that."

"I think it very unlikely," said Miss Camilla. "Most of them could neither read nor write, and they would hardly have understood an explanation so complex. No, it must be something else. I wonder—" She stopped short and stood thinking intently a moment while her visitors watched her anxiously. A pained and troubled expression had crept into her usually peaceful face, and she seemed to be reviewing memories that caused her sorrow.

"Can you get the original paper for me?" she suddenly exclaimed in great excitement. "Now—at once? I have just thought of something."

"I'll get it!" cried Sally, and she was out of the house in an instant, flying swift-footed over the ground that separated them from the entrance of the cave by the river. While she was gone Miss Camilla sat silent, inwardly reviewing her painful memories.

In ten minutes Sally was back, breathless, with the precious, rusty tin box clasped in her hand. Opening it, she gave the contents to Miss Camilla, who stared at it for three long minutes in silence.

When she looked up her eyes were tragic. But she only said very quietly:

"It is my brother's writing!"

CHAPTER XII

LIGHT DAWNS ON MISS CAMILLA

"WHAT do you make of it all, Sally?"

The two girls were sitting in the pine grove on the heights of Slipper Point. They sat each with her back against a tree and with the enchanting view of the upper river spread out panoramically before them. Each of them was knitting,—an accomplishment they had both recently acquired.

"I can't make anything of it at all, and I've thought of it day and night ever since," was Sally's reply. "It's three weeks now since the day we came through that tunnel and discovered where it ended. And except what Miss Camilla told us that day, she's never mentioned a thing about it since."

"It's strange, how she stopped short, just after she'd said the writing was her brother's," mused Doris. "And then asked us in the next breath not to question her about it any more, and to forgive her silence in the matter because it probably concerned something that was painful to her."

"Yes, and kept the paper we found in the cave," went on Sally. "I believe she wanted to study it out and see what she could make of it. If she's sure it was written by her brother, she will probably be able to puzzle it out better than we would. One thing, I guess, is certain, though. It isn't any secret directions where to find treasure. All our little hopes about that turned out very differently, didn't they?"

"Sally, are you glad or sorry we've discovered what we did about that cave?" demanded Doris suddenly.

"Oh, glad, of course," was Sally's reply. "At first, I was awfully disgusted to think all my plans and hopes about it and finding buried treasure and all that had come to nothing. But, do you know what has made me feel differently about it?" She looked up quickly at Doris.

"No, what?" asked her companion curiously.

"It's Miss Camilla herself," answered Sally. "I used to think you were rather silly to be so crazy about her and admire her so much. I'd never thought anything about her and I'd known her 'most all my life. But since she asked us that day to come and see her as often as we liked and stop at her house whenever we were up this way, and consider her as our friend, I've somehow come to feel differently. I'm glad we took her at her word and did it. I don't think I would have, if it hadn't been for you. But you've insisted on our stopping at her house so frequently, and we've become so well acquainted with her that I really think I—I almost—love her."

It pleased Doris beyond words to hear Sally make this admission. She wanted Sally to appreciate all that was fine and admirable and lovely in Miss Camilla, even if she were poor and lonely and deaf. She felt that the friendship would be good for Sally, and she knew that she herself was profiting by the increased acquaintance with this friend they had so strangely made.

"Wasn't it nice of her to teach us to knit?" went on Sally. "She said we all ought to be doing it now to help out our soldiers, since the country is at war."

"She's taught me lots beside that," said Doris. "I just love to hear her talk about old potteries and porcelains and that sort of thing. I do believe she knows more about them than even grandfather does. She's making me crazy to begin a collection myself some day when I'm old enough. She must have had a fine collection once. I do wonder what became of it."

"Well, I don't understand much about all that talk," admitted Sally. "I never saw any porcelains worth while in all my life, except that little thing she has on her mantel. And I don't see anything to get so crazy about in that. It's kind of pretty, of course, but why get excited about it? What puzzles me more is why she never has said what became of all her other things."

"That's a part of the mystery," said Doris. "And her brother's mixed up in it somehow, and perhaps her father. That much I'm sure of. She talks freely enough about everything else except those things, so that must be it. Do you know what I'm almost tempted to think? That her brother *did* commit some crime, and her father hid him away in the cave to escape from justice, but she couldn't have known about it, that's plain. Because she did not know about the cave and tunnel at all till just lately. Perhaps she wondered what became of him. And maybe they sold all her lovely porcelains to make up for what he'd done somehow."

"Yes," cried Sally in sudden excitement. "And another idea has just come to me. Maybe that queer paper was a note her brother left for her and she can't make out how to read it. Did you ever think of that?"

"Why, no!" exclaimed Doris, struck with the new idea. "I never thought of it as anything he might have left for *her*. Do you remember, she said once they were awfully fond of each other, more even than most brothers and sisters? It would be perfectly natural if he *did* want to leave her a note, if he had to go away and perhaps never come back. And of course he wouldn't want any one else to understand what it said. Oh, wait!—I have an idea we've never thought of before. Why on earth have we been so *stupid*!—"

She sprang up and began to walk about excitedly, while Sally watched her, consumed with curiosity. At length she could bear the suspense no longer.

"Well, for pity's sake tell me what you've thought of!" she demanded. "I'll go wild if you keep it to yourself much longer."

"Where's that copy?" was all Doris would reply. "I want to study it a moment." Sally drew it from her pocket and handed it to her, and Doris spent another five minutes regarding it absorbedly.

"It is. It surely is!" she muttered, half to herself. "But how are we ever going to think out how to work it?" At last she turned to the impatient Sally.

"I'm a fool not to have thought of this before, Sally. I read a book once,—I can't think what it was now, but it was some detective story,—where there was something just a little like this. Not that it looked like this, but the idea was the same. If it is what I think, it isn't the note itself at all. The note, if there is one, must be somewhere else. This is only a secret *code*, or arrangement of the letters, so that one can read the note by it. Probably the real note is written in such a way that it could never be understood at all without this. Do you understand?"

Sally had indeed grasped the idea and was wildly excited by it.

"Oh, Doris," she cried admiringly. "You certainly *are* a wonder to have thought all this out! It's ten times as interesting as what we first thought it was. But how do you work this code? I can't make anything out of it at all."

"Well, neither can I, I'll have to admit. But here's what I *think*. If we could see what that note itself looks like, we could perhaps manage to puzzle out just how this code works."

"But how are we going to do that?" demanded Doris. "Only Miss Camilla has the note, if there *is* a *note*; and certainly we couldn't very well ask her to let us see it, especially after what she said to us that day."

"No, we couldn't, I suppose," said Doris, thoughtfully. "And yet—" she hesitated. "I somehow feel perfectly certain that Miss Camilla doesn't know the meaning of all this yet, hasn't even guessed what we have, about this paper. She doesn't act so. Maybe she doesn't even know there *is* a note,—you can't tell. If she hasn't guessed, it would be a mercy to tell her, wouldn't it?"

"Yes, I suppose so," admitted Sally dubiously. "But I wouldn't know how to go about it. Would you?"

"I could only try and do my best, and beg her to forgive me if I were intruding," said Doris. "Yes, I believe she ought to be told. You can't tell how she may be worrying about all this. She acts awfully worried, seems to me. Not at all like she did when we first knew her. I believe we ought to tell her right now. Call Genevieve and we'll go over."

Sally called to Genevieve, who was playing in the boat on the beach below, and that young lady soon came scrambling up the bank. Hand in hand, all three started to the home of Miss Camilla and when they had reached it, found her sitting on her tiny porch knitting in apparently placid content. But, true to Doris's observation, there were anxious lines in her face that had not been seen a month ago. She greeted them, however, with real pleasure, and with her usual hospitality proffered refreshments, this time in the shape of some early peaches she had gathered only that morning.

But Doris who, with Sally's consent, had constituted herself spokesman, before accepting the refreshment, began:

"Miss Camilla, I wonder if you'll forgive us for speaking of something to you? It may seem as if we were intruding, but we really don't intend to."

"Why, speak right on," exclaimed that lady in surprise. "You are too well-bred to be intrusive, that I know. If you feel you must speak of something to me, I know it is because you think it wise or necessary."

Much relieved by this assurance, Doris went on, explaining how she had suddenly had a new idea concerning the mysterious paper and detailing what she thought it might be. As she proceeded, a new light of comprehension seemed to creep into the face of Miss Camilla, who had been listening intently.

"So we think it must be a code,—a secret code,—Miss Camilla. And if you happen to have any queer sort of note or communication that you've never been able to make out, why this may explain it," she added.

When she had finished, Miss Camilla sat perfectly still—thinking. She thought so long and so intently that it seemed as if she must have forgotten completely the presence of the three on the porch with her. And after what seemed an interminable period, she did a strange thing. Instead of replying with so much as a word, she got up and went into the house, leaving them open-mouthed and wondering.

"Do you suppose she's angry with us?" whispered Sally. "Do you think we ought to stay?"

"No, I don't think she's angry," replied Doris in a low voice. "I think she's so—so absorbed that she hardly realizes what she's doing or that we are here. We'd better stay."

They stayed. But so long was Miss Camilla gone that even Doris began to doubt the wisdom of remaining any longer.

But presently she came back. Her recently neat dress was grimy and dishevelled. There was a streak of dust across her face and a cobweb lay on her hair. Doris guessed at once that she had been in the old, unused portion of her house. But in her hand she carried something, and resuming her seat, she laid it carefully on her knee. It was a little book about four inches wide and six or seven long, with an old-fashioned brown cover, and it was coated with what seemed to be the dust of years. The two girls gazed at it curiously, and when Miss Camilla had got her breath, she explained:

"I can never thank you enough for what you have told me today. It throws light on something that has never been clear to me,—something that I have even forgotten for long years. If what you surmise is true, then a mystery that has surrounded my life for more than fifty years will be at last explained. It is strange that the idea did not occur to me when first you girls discovered the cave and the tunnel, but even then it remained unconnected in my mind with—*this*." She pointed to the little book in her lap. Then she went on:

"But, now, under the circumstances, I feel that I must explain it all to you, relying still on your discretion and secrecy. For I have come to know that you are both unusually trustworthy young folks. There has been a dark shadow over my life,—a darker shadow than you can perhaps imagine. I told you before of my father's opinions and leanings during the years preceding the Civil War. When that terrible conflict broke out, he insisted that I go away to Europe with my aunt and stay there as long as it lasted, providing me with ample funds to do so. I think that he did not believe at first that the struggle would be so long.

"I went with considerable reluctance, but I was accustomed to obeying his wishes implicitly. I was gone two years, and in all that time I received the most loving and affectionate letters constantly, both from him and also my brother. They assured me that everything was well with them. My brother had enlisted at once in the Union Army and had fought through a number of campaigns. My father remained here, but was doing his utmost, so he said, in a private capacity, to further the interests of the country. Altogether, their reports were glowing. And though I was often worried as to the outcome, and apprehensive for my brother's safety, I spent the two years abroad very happily.

"Then, in May of 1863, my first calamity happened. My aunt died very suddenly and unexpectedly, while we were in Switzerland, and, as we had been alone, it was my sad duty to bring her back to New York. After her funeral, I hurried home here, wondering very much that my father had not come on to be with me, for I had sent him word immediately upon my arrival. My brother, I suspected, was away with the army.

"I was completely astounded and dismayed, on arriving home, at the condition of affairs I found here. To begin with, there were no servants about. Where they had gone, or why they had been dismissed, I could not discover. My father was alone in his study when I arrived, which was rather late in the evening. He was reserved and rather taciturn in his greeting to me, and did not act very much pleased to welcome me back. This grieved me greatly, after my long absence. But I could see that he was worried and preoccupied and in trouble of some kind. I thought that perhaps he had had bad news about my brother Roland, but he assured me that Roland was all right.

"Then I asked him why the house was in such disorder and where the servants were, but he only begged me not to make inquiries about that matter at present, but to go to my room and make myself as comfortable as I could, and he would explain it all later. I did as he asked me and went to my room. I had been there about an hour, busying myself with unpacking my bag, when there was a hurried knock at my door. I went to open it, and gave a cry of joy, for there stood my brother Roland.

"Instead of greeting me, however, he seized my hand and cried: 'Father is very ill. He has had some sort of a stroke. Hurry downstairs to him at once. I must leave immediately. I can't even wait to see how he is. It is imperative!'

" 'But, Roland,' I cried, 'surely you won't go leaving Father like this!' But he only answered, 'I must. I must! It's my duty!' He seized me in his arms and kissed me, and was gone without another word. But before he went, I had seen—a dreadful thing! He was enveloped from head to foot in a long, dark military cape of some kind, reaching almost to his feet. But as he embraced me under the light of the hall lamp, the cloak was thrown aside for an instant and I had that terrible glimpse. Under the concealing cloak my brother was wearing a uniform of *Confederate gray*.

"I almost fainted at the sight, but he was gone before I could utter a word, without probably even knowing that I *had* seen. This, then, was the explanation of the mysterious way they had treated me. They had gone over to the enemy. They were traitors to their country and their faith, and they did not want me to know. For this they had even sent me away out of the country!...

"But I had no time to think about that then. I hurried to my father and found him on the couch in his study, inert in the grip of a paralytic stroke that had deprived him of the use of his limbs and also of coherent speech. I spent the rest of the night trying to make him easier, but the task was difficult. I had no one to send for a doctor and could not leave him to go myself, and of course the nearest doctor was several miles away. There was not even a neighbor who could be called upon for assistance.

"All that night, however, my father tried to tell me something. His speech was almost absolutely incoherent, but several times I caught the sound of words like 'notebook' and 'explain.' But I could make nothing of it. In the early morning another stroke took him, and he passed away very quietly in my arms.

"I can scarcely bear, even now, to recall the days that followed. After the funeral, I retired very much into myself and saw almost no one. I felt cut off and abandoned by all humanity. I did not know where my brother was, could not even communicate with him about the death of our father. Had he been in the Union Army I would have inquired. But the glimpse I had had that night of his rebel uniform was sufficient to seal my lips forever. There was no one in the village whom I knew well enough to discuss any such matters with, nor any remaining relative with whom I was in sympathy. I could only wait for my brother's return to solve the mystery.

"But my brother never returned. In all these years I have neither seen him nor heard of him, and I know beyond doubt that he is long since dead. And I have remained here by myself like a hermit, because I feel that the shame of it all has hung about me and enveloped me, and I cannot get away from it. Once, a number of years ago, an old village gossip here, now long since gone, said to me, 'There was something queer about your father and brother, now wasn't there, Miss Camilla? I've heard tell as how they were "Rebs" on the quiet, during the big war awhile back. Is that so?' Of course, the chance remark only served to confirm the suspicions in my mind, though I denied it firmly to her when she said it.

"I also found to my amazement, when I went over the house after all was over, that many things I had loved and valued had strangely disappeared. All the family silver, of which we had had a valuable set inherited from Revolutionary forefathers, was gone. Some antique jewelry that I had picked up abroad and prized highly was also missing. But chief of all, my whole collection of precious porcelains and pottery was nowhere to be found. I searched in every conceivable nook and cranny in vain. And at last the disagreeable truth was forced on me that my father and brother had sold or disposed of them, for what ends I could not guess. But it only added to my bitterness to think they could do such a despicable thing without so much as consulting me.

"But now, at last, I come to the notebook. I found it among some papers in my father's study desk, a while after his death, and I frankly confess I could make nothing of it whatever. It seemed to be filled with figures, added and subtracted, and, as my father had always been rather fond of dabbling with figures and mathematics, I put it down as being some quiet calculations of his own that had no bearing on anything concerning me. I laid it carefully away with his other papers, however, and there it has been, in an old trunk in the attic of the unused part all these years. When you spoke of a 'secret code,' however, it suddenly occurred to me that the notebook might be concerned in the matter. Here it is."

She held it out to them and they crowded about her eagerly. But as she laid it open and they examined its pages, a disappointed look crept into Sally's eyes.

"Why, there's nothing here but *numbers*!" she exclaimed, and it was even so. The first few lines were as follows:

56 + 14 - 63 + 43 + 34 + 54 + 64 + 43 +

16 - 52 + 66 + 52 + 15 + 23 - 66 + 24 -

15 + 44 + 43 - 43 + 64 + 43 + 24 + 15 -

61 + 53 - 36 + 24 + 14 - 51 + 15 + 53 +

54 + 43 + 52 + 43 + 43 + 15 - 16 + 66 +

52 + 36 + 52 + 15 + 43 + 23 -

And all the rest were exactly like them in character.

But Doris, who had been quietly examining it, with a copy of the code in her other hand, suddenly uttered a delighted cry:

"I have it! At least, I *think* I'm on the right track. Just examine this code a moment, Miss Camilla. If you notice, leaving out the line of figures at the top and right of the whole square, the rest is just the letters of

"Why, there's nothing there but numbers"

the alphabet and the figures one to nine and another 'o' that probably stands for 'naught.' There are six squares across and six squares down, and those numbers on the outside are just one to six, only all mixed up. Don't you see how it could be worked? Suppose one wanted to write the letter 't.' It could be indicated by the number '5' (meaning the square it comes under according to the top line of figures) and '1' (the number according to the side line). Then '51' would stand for letter 'T,' wouldn't it?"

“Great!” interrupted Sally, enthusiastically, who had seen the method even quicker than Miss Camilla. “But suppose it worked the other way, reading the side line first? Then ‘T’ would be ‘15.’ ”

“Of course, that’s true,” admitted Doris. “I suppose there must have been some understanding between those who invented this code about which line to read first. The only way we can discover it is to puzzle it out both ways, and see which makes sense. One will and the other won’t.”

It all seemed as simple as rolling off a log, now that Doris had discovered the explanation. Even Miss Camilla was impressed with the value of the discovery.

“But what is the meaning of these plus and minus signs?” she queried. “I suppose they stand for something.”

“I think that’s easy,” answered Doris. “In looking over it, I see there are a great many more plus than minus signs. Now, I think the plus signs must be intended to divide the numbers in groups of two, so that each group stands for a letter. Otherwise they’d be all hopelessly mixed up. And the minus signs divide the words. And every once in a while, if you notice, there’s a multiplication sign. I imagine those as the periods at the end of sentences.”

They all sat silent a moment after this, marveling at the simplicity of it. But at length Doris suggested:

“Suppose we try to puzzle out a little of it and see if we are really on the right track? Have you a piece of paper and a pencil, Miss Camilla?” Miss Camilla went indoors and brought them out, quivering with the excitement of the new discovery.

“Now, let’s see,” began Doris. “Suppose we try reading the top line first. ‘56’ would be ‘1’ and ‘14’ would be ‘2.’ Now ‘12’ may mean a word or it may not. It hardly seems as if a note would begin with that. Let’s try it the other way. Side line first. Then ‘56’ is ‘m,’ and ‘14’ is ‘y.’ ‘*My*’ is a word, anyway, so perhaps we’re on the right track. Let’s go on.”

From the next series of letters she spelled the word “beloved” and after that “sister.” It was plain beyond all doubting that at last they had stumbled on a wonderful discovery.

But she got no further than the words, “my beloved sister,” for, no sooner had Miss Camilla taken in their meaning than she huddled back in her chair and, very quietly, fainted away.

CHAPTER XIII

WORD FROM THE PAST

NONE of the three had ever seen any one unconscious before. Sally stood back, aghast and helpless. Genevieve expressed herself as she usually did in emergencies, with a loud and resounding howl. But Doris rushed into the house, fetched a dipper of cold water and dashed it into Miss Camilla’s face. Then she began to rub her hands and ordered Sally to fan her as hard as she could. The simple expedients worked in a short time, and Miss Camilla came to herself.

“I—I never did such a foolish thing before!” she gasped, when she realized what had happened. “But this is all so—so amazing and startling! It almost seemed like my brother’s own voice, speaking to me from the past.” Again she sat back in her chair and closed her eyes, but this time only to regain her poise. And then Doris did a very tactful thing.

"Miss Camilla," she began, "we've discovered how to read the notebook, and I'm sure you won't have any trouble with it. I think we had better be getting home now, for it is nearly five o'clock. So we'll say good-bye for today, and hope you won't feel faint any more."

Miss Camilla gave her a grateful glance. Greatly as she wished to be alone with this message left her by a brother whose fate she did not dare to guess, yet she was too courteous to dismiss these two girls who had done so much toward helping her solve the problem. And she was more appreciative of Doris's thoughtful suggestion of departure than she could have put into words.

"Thank you, dear," she replied, "and come again tomorrow, all of you. Perhaps I shall have—something to tell you then!"

And with many a backward glance and much waving of hands, they took their departure across the fields.

. . . .

It was with the wildest impatience that they waited for the following afternoon to obey Miss Camilla's behest and "come again." But promptly at two o'clock they were trailing through the pine woods and the meadow that separated it from the Roundtree farmhouse.

"Do you know," whispered Sally, "crazy as I am to hear all about it, I almost dread it, too. I'm so afraid it may have been bad news for her."

"I feel just the same," confided Doris, "and yet I'm bursting with impatience, too. Well, let's go on and hear the worst. If it's very bad, she probably won't want to say much about it."

But their first sight of Miss Camilla convinced them that the news was not, at least, "very bad." She sat on the porch as usual, knitting serenely, but there was a new light in her face, a sweet, satisfied tranquillity that had never been there before.

"I'm glad you've come!" she greeted them. "I have much to tell you."

"Was it—was it all right?" faltered Doris.

"It was more than 'all right,' " she replied. "It was wonderful. But I am going to read the whole thing to you. I spent nearly all last night deciphering the letter,—for a letter it was,—and I think it is only right you should hear it, after what you have done for me." She went inside the house and brought out several large sheets of paper on which she had transcribed the meaning of the mysterious message.

"Listen," she said. "It is as wonderful as a fairy-tale. And how I have misjudged him!"

" 'My beloved sister,' " she read, " 'in the event of any disaster befalling us, I want you to know the danger and the difficulties of what we have undertaken. It is only right that you should, and I know of no other way to communicate it to you, than by the roundabout means of this military cipher which I am using. You are away in Europe now, and safe, and Father intentionally keeps you there because of the very dangerous enterprise in which we are involved. Lest any untoward thing should befall before your return, we leave this as an explanation.

" 'Contrary to any appearances, or anything you may hear said in the future, I am a loyal and devoted soldier of the Union. But I am serving it in the most dangerous capacity imaginable,—as a scout or spy in the Confederate Army, wearing its uniform, serving in its ranks, but in reality spying on every move and action and communicating all its secrets that I am capable of obtaining to the Government and our own commanders. I stand in hourly danger of being discovered—and for that there is but one end. You know what it is. Of course, I am not serving under my own name, so that if you never hear word of my fate, you may know it is the only one possible for those who are serving as I serve.

" 'Father is also carrying on the work, but in a slightly different capacity. There are a set of Confederate workers up here secretly engaged in raising funds and planning new campaigns for the South. Father has identified himself with them, and they hold many meetings at our house to discuss plans and information. Apparently he is hand in glove with them, but in reality is all the while disclosing their plans to the Government. They could doubtless kill him without scruple, if they suspected it, and get away to the safety of their own lines unscathed, before anything was discovered. So you see, he also stands hourly on the brink of death.

" 'For two years we have carried on this work unharmed, but I suppose it cannot go on forever. Some day my disguise will be penetrated, and all will be over with me. Some day Father will meet with some violent end when he is alone and unprotected, and no one will be found to answer for the deed. But it will all be for the glory of the Union we delight to serve. Now do you understand the situation?

" 'I do not get home here often, and never except for the purpose of conveying some message that will best be sent to headquarters through this channel. My field of service is with the armies south of the Potomac. But while I am here now, Father and I have consulted as to the best way of communicating this news to you and have decided on this means. We cannot tell how soon our end may come. Father tells me there are rumors about here that we are serving the Confederate side. Should you return unexpectedly and find us gone, and perhaps hear those rumors, you would certainly be justified in putting the worst construction on our actions.

" 'So we have decided to write and leave you this message. It will be left carelessly among Father's papers, and without the cipher will, of course, be unreadable by any one. But we have not yet decided in what place to conceal the cipher where there is no danger of its being discovered. That is a military secret and, if it were disclosed, would be fatal and far-reaching in its consequences.' "

Miss Camilla stopped there, and her spellbound listeners drew a long breath.

"Isn't it wonderful!" breathed Doris. "And they were loyal and devoted to the Union all the time. How happy you must be, Miss Camilla."

"I am happy,—beyond words!" she replied. "But that is not quite all of it. So far, it was evidently written at one sitting, calmly and coherently. There is a little more, but it is hasty and confused, and somewhat puzzling. It must have been added at another time, and I suspect now, probably just at the time of my return. There is a blank half-page, and then it goes on:

" 'In a great hurry. Most vital and urgent business has brought me back to see Father. Just learned you were here. There is grave, terrible danger. The rebels are invading. I am with them, of course. Not far away. Must return tonight, at once, to lines, if I ever get there alive. Have a task before me that will undoubtedly see the end of me. In this rig and in this place am open to danger from friend and foe alike. But there is no time to change. Hope for best. Forgive haste but there is not a moment to lose. Father seems ill and unlike himself. He saw two or three Confederate spies at the house today. Always suspect something is wrong after such a meeting. Don't be surprised at state of the house. Unavoidable but all right. Father will explain where I have hidden this cipher code. Always your loving brother,

" 'Roland.'

"And there is one more strange line," ended Miss Camilla. "It is this:

" 'In case you should forget, or Father doesn't tell you, right hand side from house, behind 27.' "

"That is all!" She folded up the paper and sat looking away over the meadow, as did the others, in the awed silence that followed naturally the receipt of this message of one whose fate could be only too well guessed.

"And he never came back?" half-whispered Doris, at last.

"No, he never came back," answered Miss Camilla softly. "I haven't a doubt but that he met the fate he so surely predicted. I have been thinking back and reading back over the events of that period, and I can pretty well reconstruct what must have happened. It was in the month of June of 1863, when Lee suddenly invaded Pennsylvania. From that time until his defeat at Gettysburg, there was the greatest panic all through this region, and every one was certain that it spelt ruin for the entire North, especially Pennsylvania and New Jersey. I suppose my brother was with his army and had made his way over home here to get or communicate news. How he came or went, I cannot imagine, and never shall know. But I can easily see how his fate would be certain were he seen by any of the Federal authorities in a Confederate uniform. Probably no explanation would save him, with many of them. For that was the risk run by every scout, to be the prey of friend and foe alike, unless he could get hold of the highest authority in time. He doubtless lies in an unknown grave, either in this state or in Pennsylvania."

"But—your father?" hesitated Sally. "Do you—do you think anything queer—happened to him?"

"That I shall never know either," answered Miss Camilla. "His symptoms looked to me like apoplexy, at the time. Now that I think it over, they might possibly have been caused by some slow and subtle poison having a gradually paralyzing effect. You see, my brother says he had seen some of the Confederate spies that day. Perhaps they had begun to suspect him, and had taken this means to get him out of the way. I cannot tell. As I could not get a doctor at the time, the village doctor, who had known us all our lives, took my word for it next day that it was apoplexy. But, whatever it may have been, I know that they both died in the service of the country they loved, and that is enough for me. It has removed the burden of many years of grief and shame from my shoulders. I can once more lift up my head among my fellow-countrymen!"

And Miss Camilla did actually radiate happiness with her whole attractive personality.

"But I cannot make any meaning out of that queer last line," mused Sally after a time. "Will you read it to us again, Miss Camilla, please?"

And Miss Camilla repeated the odd message,—" 'In case you should forget, or Father does not tell you, right hand side from house, behind twenty-seven.' "

"Now what in the world can that all mean?" she demanded. "At first I thought perhaps it might mean where they had hidden the code, but that couldn't be because we found that under the old mattress in the cave. Your brother probably went out that way that night and left it there on the way."

"Wait a minute," suddenly interrupted Doris. "Do you remember just before the end he says, 'do not be surprised at the state of the house. Unavoidable but all right.' Now what could he mean by *that*? Do you know what I think? I believe he was apologizing because things seemed so upset and—and many of the valuable things were missing, as Miss Camilla said. If there was such excitement about, and fear of Lee's invasion, why isn't it possible that they *hid* those valuable things somewhere, so they would be safe, whatever happened, and this was to tell her, without speaking too plainly, that it was all right? The brother thought his father would explain, but in case he didn't, or it was forgotten, he gave the clue where to find them."

Miss Camilla sat forward in renewed excitement, her eye-glasses brushed awry. "Why, of course! Of course! I've never thought of it. Not once since I read this letter. The other was so much more important. But naturally that is what they must have done,—hidden them to keep them safe. They never, never would have disposed of them in any other way or for any other reason. But where in the world can that place be? 'Right hand side from the house behind 27' means nothing at all—to me!"

"Well, it does to *me*!" suddenly exclaimed Sally, the natural-born treasure-hunter of them all. "Where else *could* they hide anything so safely as in that cave or tunnel? Nobody would ever suspect in the world. And I somehow don't think it meant the cave. I believe it means somewhere in the tunnel, on the right hand side as you enter from the cellar."

"But what about 27?" demanded Miss Camilla. "That doesn't seem to mean anything, does it?"

"No, of course it doesn't mean anything to you, because you haven't been through the tunnel, and wouldn't know. But every once in a while, along the sides, are planks from that old vessel, put there to keep the sides more firm, I guess. There must be seventy-five or a hundred on each side. Now I believe it means that if we look behind the twenty-seventh one from the cellar entrance, on the right hand side, we'll find the—the things hidden there."

Then Miss Camilla rose, the light of younger days shining adventurously in her eyes.

"If that's the case, we'll go and dig them out tomorrow!" she announced gaily.

CHAPTER XIV

THE REAL BURIED TREASURE

IT had been a very dull day indeed for Genevieve. Had she been able to communicate her feelings adequately, she would have said she was heartily sick and tired of the program she had been obliged to follow. As she sat solitary on the porch of Miss Camilla's tiny abode, thumb in mouth and tugging at the lock of hair with her other hand, she thought it all over resentfully.

Why should she be commanded to sit here all by herself, in a spot that offered no attractions whatever, told, nay, *commanded* not to move from the location, when she was bored beyond expression by the entire proceeding? True, they had left her eatables in generous quantities, but she had already disposed of these, and as for the picture-books of many attractive descriptions, given her to while away the weary hours, they were an old story now, and the afternoon was growing late. She longed to go down to the shore and play in the rowboat, and dabble her bare toes in the water, and indulge in the eternally fascinating experiment of catching crabs with a piece of meat tied to a string and her father's old crab-net. What was the use of living when one was doomed to drag out a wonderful afternoon on a tiny, hopelessly uninteresting porch out in the backwoods? Existence was nothing but a burden.

True, the morning had not been without its pleasant moments. They had rowed up the river to their usual landing-place, a trip she always enjoyed, though it had been somewhat marred by the fear that she might be again compelled to burrow into the earth like a mole, forsaking the glory of sunshine and sparkling water for the dismal dampness of that unspeakable hole in the ground. But, to her immense relief, this sacrifice was not required of her. Instead, they had made at once through the woods and across the fields to Miss

Camilla's, albeit burdened with many strange and, to her mind, useless tools and other impedimenta.

Miss Camilla's house offered attractions not a few, chiefly in the way of unlimited cookies and other eatables. But her enjoyment of the cookies was tempered by the fact that the whole party suddenly took it into their heads to proceed to the cellar and, what was even worse, to attempt again the loathsome undertaking of scrambling through the narrow place in the wall and the journey beyond. She herself accompanied them as far as the cellar, but further than that she refused to budge. So they left her in the cellar with a candle and a seat conveniently near a barrel of apples.

It amazed her, moreover, that a person of Miss Camilla's years and sense should engage in this foolish escapade. She had learned to expect nothing better of Sally and "Dowis," but that Miss Camilla herself should descend enthusiastically to so senseless a performance, caused her somewhat of a shock. She had not expected it of Miss Camilla.

It transpired, however, that they did not proceed far into the tunnel. She could hear them talking and exclaiming excitedly, and discussing whether "this was really twenty-seven," and "hadn't we better count again," and "shall we saw it out," and other equally pointless remarks of a similar nature. Wearying of listening to such idle chatter, and replete with cookies and russet apples, she had finally put her head down on the edge of the barrel and had fallen fast asleep.

When she had awakened, it was to find them all back in the cellar, and Miss Camilla making the pleasant announcement that "they would have luncheon now and get to work in earnest afterward." A soul-satisfying interval followed, the only really bright spot in the day for Genevieve. But gloom had settled down upon her once more when they had risen from the table. Solemnly they had taken her on their laps (at least Miss Camilla had!) and ominously Sally had warned her:

"Now, Genevieve, we've got something awfully important to do this afternoon. You don't like to go down in that dark place, so we've decided not to take you with us. You'd rather stay up here in the sunshine, wouldn't you?" And she had nodded vigorously an unqualified assent to that proposition. "Well, then," Sally had continued, "you stay right on this porch or in the sitting-room, and don't you dare venture a foot away from it. Will you promise?" Again Genevieve had nodded. "Nothing will hurt you if you mind what we say, and by and by we'll come back and show you something awfully nice." Genevieve had seriously doubted the possibility of this latter statement, but she was helpless in their hands.

"And here's plenty of cookies and a glass of jam," Miss Camilla had supplemented, "and we'll come back to you soon, you blessed baby!" Then they had all hugged and kissed her and departed.

Well, they had not kept their word. She had heard the little clock in the room within, strike and strike and strike, sometimes just one bell-like tone, sometimes two and three and four. She could not yet "tell the time" but she knew enough about a clock to realize that this indicated the passing of the moments. And still there had been no sign of return on the part of the exploring three.

Genevieve whimpered a little and wiped her eyes, sad to say, on her sleeve. Then she thrust her hand, for the fortieth time into the cooky-jar. But it was empty. And then, in sheer boredom and despair, she put her head down on the arm of her chair, tucked her thumb into her mouth and closed her eyes to shut out the tiresome scene before her. In this position she had remained what seemed a long, long time, and the clock had sounded another bell-like stroke, when she was suddenly aroused by a sound quite different.

At first she did not give it much thought, but it came again louder this time, and she sat up with a jerk. Was some one calling her? It was a strange, muffled sound, and it seemed as if it were like a voice trying to pronounce her name.

"Genev—! Genev—!" That was all she could distinguish. Did they want her, possibly to go down into the horrible cellar and hole? She went to the door giving on the cellar steps and listened. But, though she stood there fully five minutes, she heard not so much as a breath. No, it could not be that. She would go out doors again.

But, no sooner had she stepped onto the porch than she heard it again, fainter this time, but undeniable. Where *could* it come from? They had commanded her not to venture a step from the porch but surely, if they were calling her she ought to try and find them. So she stepped down from the veranda and ran around to the back of the house. This time she was rewarded. The sound came clearer and more forcefully:

"Genevieve!—Genev—ieve!" But where, still, could it come from? There was not a soul in sight. The garden (for it was Miss Camilla's vegetable garden) was absolutely deserted of human occupation. But Genevieve wisely decided to follow the sound, so she began to pick her way gingerly between the rows of beans, climbing on quite a forest of tall poles. It was when she had passed these that she came upon something that caused her a veritable shock.

The ground in Miss Camilla's cucumber patch, for the space of ten or twelve feet square, had sunk down into a strange hole, as if in a sudden earthquake. What did it all mean? And, as Genevieve hesitated on its brink, she was startled almost out of her little shoes to hear her name called faintly and in a muffled voice from its depths.

"Genev—ieve!" It was the voice of Doris, though she could see not the slightest vestige of her.

"Here I am!" answered Genevieve quaveringly. "What do you want, Dowis?"

"Oh, thank God!" came the reply. "Go get—some one. Quick. We're—buried alive! It—caved in. Hurry—baby!"

"Who s'all I get?" demanded Genevieve. And well she might ask, for as far as any one knew, there was not a soul within a mile of them.

"Oh—I don't—know!" came the answering voice. "Go find—some one. Any one. We'll die—here—if you—don't!" Genevieve was not sure she knew just what that last remark meant, but it evidently indicated something serious.

"All right!" she responded. "I will twy!" And she trotted off to the front of the house.

Here, however, she stopped to consider. Where *was* she to go to find any one? She could not go back home,—she did not know the way. She could not go back to the river,—the way was full of pitfalls in the shape of thorny vines that scratched her face and tripped her feet, and besides, Sally had particularly warned her not to venture in that direction—ever. After all, the most likely place to find any one was surely along the road, for she had, very rarely when sitting on Miss Camilla's porch, observed a wagon driven past. She would walk along the road and see if she could find anybody.

Had Genevieve been older and with a little more understanding, she would have comprehended the desperate plight that had befallen her sister and Doris and Miss Camilla. And she would have lent wings to her feet and scurried to the nearest dwelling as fast as those feet would carry her. But she was scarcely more than a baby. The situation, though peculiar, did not strike her as so much a matter for haste as for patient waiting till the person required should happen along. As she didn't see any one approaching in either direction, she decided to return to the house and keep a strict eye on the road.

And so she returned, seated herself on the porch steps, tucked her thumb in her mouth—and waited. There was no further calling from the curious hole in the back garden and nothing happened for a long, long time. Genevieve had just about decided to go back and inquire of Doris what else to do, when suddenly the afternoon stillness was broken by the "chug-chug" of a motor car and the honking of its horn. And before Genevieve could jump to her feet, a big automobile had come plowing down the sandy road and stopped right in front of the gate.

"Here's the place!" called out the chauffeur, and jumping down, walked around to open the door at the side for its occupants to get out. A pleasant-looking man descended and gave his hand to the lady beside him. And, to Genevieve's great astonishment, the lady proved to be none other than the mother of "Dowis."

"Well, where's every one?" inquired the gentleman. "I don't see a soul but this wee tot sitting on the steps."

"Why, there's Genevieve!" cried Mrs. Craig, who had seen the baby many times before. "How are you, dear? Where are the others? Inside?"

"No," answered Genevieve. "In de garden. Dowis she said come. Find some one."

"Oh, they're in the garden, are they? Well, we'll go around there and give them a surprise, Henry. Doris will simply be bowled over to see her 'daddy' here so unexpectedly! And I'm very anxious to meet this Miss Camilla she has talked so much about. Come and show us the way, Genevieve."

The baby obediently took her hand and led her around to the back of the house, the gentleman following.

"But I don't see any one here!" he exclaimed when they had reached the back. "Aren't you mistaken, honey?" This to Genevieve.

"No, they in big hole," she announced gravely. The remark aroused considerable surprise and amused curiosity.

"Well, lead us to the 'big hole,' " commanded Mrs. Craig laughingly. "Big hole, indeed! I've been wondering what in the world Doris was up to lately, but I never dreamed she was excavating!"

Genevieve still gravely led the way through the forest of bean-poles to the edge of the newly sunk depression.

"What's all this?" suddenly demanded Mr. Craig. "It looks as if there had been a landslide here. Where are the others, little girl? They've probably forsaken this and gone elsewhere."

But Genevieve was not to be moved from her original statement. "They in dere!" she insisted, pointing downward. "Dowis called. She say 'Go find some one.' " The baby's persistence was not to be questioned.

Mr. Craig looked grave and his wife grew pale and frightened. "Oh, Henry, what do you suppose can be the matter?" she quavered. "I do believe Genevieve is telling the truth."

"There's something mighty queer about it," he answered hastily. "I can't understand how in the world it has come about, but if that child is right, there's been a landslide or a cave-in of some sort here and Doris and the rest are caught in it. Good heavens! If that's so, we can't act too quickly!" and he ran round to the front of the house shouting to the chauffeur, who had remained in the car:

"There's been an accident. Drive like mad to the nearest house and get men and ropes and spades,—anything to help dig out some people from a cave-in!" The car had shot down the road almost before he had ceased speaking, and he hurried back to the garden.

The next hour was a period of indescribable suspense and terror to all concerned,—all, at least, save Genevieve, who sat placidly on Mrs. Craig's lap (Mr. Craig had brought out a chair from Miss Camilla's kitchen) and, thumb in mouth, watched the men furiously hurling the soil in great shovelfuls from the curious "hole." She could not understand why Mrs. Craig should sob softly, at intervals, under her breath, nor why the strange gentleman should pace back and forth so restlessly and give such sharp, hurried orders. And when he jumped into the hole, with a startled exclamation, and seized the end of a heavy plank, she wondered at the unnecessary excitement.

It took the united efforts of every man present to move that plank, and when they had forced it aside, Mr. Craig stooped down with a smothered cry.

And the next thing Genevieve knew, they had lifted out some one and laid her on the ground, inert, lifeless and so covered with dirt and sand as to be scarcely recognizable. But from the light, golden hair, Genevieve knew it to be Doris. Before she knew where she was, Genevieve found herself cascaded from Mrs. Craig's lap, and that lady bending distractedly over the prostrate form.

Again the men emerged from the pit, carrying between them another form which they laid beside Doris. And, with a howl of anguish, Genevieve recognized the red-bronze pig-tail of her sister, Sally.

By the time Miss Camilla had been extricated from the débris as lifeless and inert as the other two, the chauffeur had returned at mad speed from the village, bringing with him a doctor and many strange appliances for resuscitation. A pulmotor was put into immediate action, and another period of heartbreaking suspense ensued.

It was Doris who first moaned her way back to life and at the physician's orders was carried back into the house for further ministrations. Sally was the next to show signs of recovery, but over poor Miss Camilla they had to work hard and long, for, in addition to having been almost smothered, her foot had been caught by the falling plank and badly injured. But she came back to consciousness at last, and her first words on opening her eyes were:

"Do you think we can get that Spode dinner-set out all right?" A remark which greatly bewildered Mr. Craig, who happened to be the only one to hear it!

. . . .

"But how on earth did you and Mother happen to be there, Father, just in the nick of time?" marveled Doris from the depths of several pillows with which she was propped up in bed.

She had been detailing to her parents, at great length, the whole story of Sally and the cave and the tunnel and Miss Camilla and the hazardous treasure-hunt that had ended her adventure. And now it was her turn to be enlightened.

"Well," returned her father, smiling whimsically, "it was a good deal like what they call 'the long arm of coincidence' in story-books, and yet it was very simple, after all! I'd been disappointed so many times in my plans to get down here to see you and your mother, and at last the chance came, the other day, when I could make at least a flying trip, but I hadn't even time to let you know I was coming. I arrived at the hotel about lunch-time and gave your mother the surprise of her life by walking in on her unexpectedly. But I was quite disgusted not to find you anywhere about. Your mother told me how you had gone off for the day with your bosom pal, Sally, to visit a mysterious Miss Camilla, and I suggested that we take the car and go to hunt you up. As she was agreeable to the excursion we started forth, inquiring our way as we went. It was a merciful providence that got us there not a moment too soon, and if it hadn't been for that little cherubic Genevieve we would have been many minutes too late. If it hadn't been that two or three old planks had been bent over you and protected you from the worst of the earth and débris on top, and also gave you a slight space for air, I don't believe any of you would have been alive now to tell the tale! So the next time you go treasure-hunting, young lady, kindly allow your useless and insignificant dad to accompany you!" And he gave her ear a playful tweak.

"Daddy, it was awful,—simply awful when that old plank gave way and the earth came sliding down on us!" she confided to him, snuggling down in the arm he had placed around her. "At first we didn't think it would amount to much. But more and more earth came pouring down and then another plank loosened and Miss Camilla lost her footing and fell, and we couldn't make our way out past it, either direction, and still the dirt poured in all around us, and Sally and I tried to struggle up through the top, but we couldn't make any progress. And at last that third plank bent over and shut us in so we couldn't budge, and Sally and Miss Camilla didn't answer when I spoke to them, and I knew they'd fainted, and I felt as if I was going to faint too. But I called and called Genevieve and at last she answered me. And after that I didn't remember anything more!" She shuddered and hid her face in her father's sleeve. It had been a very horrible experience.

"Don't think of it any more, honey. It turned out all right, in the end. Do you know that Sally is around as well as ever, now, and came up to the hotel to inquire for you this morning? She's as strong as a little ox, that child!"

"But where is Miss Camilla?" suddenly inquired Doris. "She hurt her foot, didn't she?"

"She certainly did, but she insisted on remaining in her own home, and Sally begged her mother to be allowed to stay also with the un-detachable Genevieve, of course, and take care of her and wait on her. So there they are, and there you will proceed in the automobile, this afternoon, if you feel well enough to make the visit."

"But what about the treasure?" demanded Doris, her eyes beginning to sparkle.

"If you refer to the trunks and chests full of articles that Miss Camilla insisted that we continue to excavate from that interesting hole in her garden, you do well to speak of it as 'treasure'!" answered her father laughingly. "For beside some valuable old family silver and quite rare articles of antique jewelry, she had there a collection of china and porcelain that would send a specialist on that subject into an absolute spasm of joy. I really would not care to predict what it would be worth to any one interested in the subject.

"And you can tell your friend, Sally, of the adventurous spirit, that she's got 'Treasure Island' licked a mile (to use a very inelegant expression) and right here on her own native territory, too. I take off my hat to you both. You've done better than a couple of boys who have been playing at and hunting for pirates all their youthful days. Henceforth, when I yearn for blood-curdling adventures and hair-breadth escapes, I'll come to you two to lead the way!"

But, under all his banter, Doris knew that her father was serious in the deep interest he entertained in her strange adventure and all that it had led to.

CHAPTER XV

THE SUMMER'S END

THEY sat together in the canoe, each facing the other, Doris in the bow and Sally in the stern. A full, mid-September moon painted its rippling path on the water and picked out in silver every detail of shore and river. The air was full of the heavy scent of the pines, and the only sound was the ceaseless lap-lap of the lazy ripples at the water's edge. Doris had laid aside her paddle. Chin in hands, she was drinking in the radiance of the lovely scene.

"I simply cannot realize I am going home tomorrow and must leave all this!" she sighed at last.

Sally dipped her paddle disconsolately and answered with almost a groan:

"If it bothers *you*, how do you suppose it makes *me* feel?"

They sat together in the canoe

"We have grown close to each other, haven't we?" mused Doris. "Do you know, I never dreamed I could make so dear a friend in so short a time. I have plenty of acquaintances and good comrades, but usually it takes me years to make a real *friend*. How did you manage to make me care so much for you, Sally?"

" 'Just because you're you'!" laughed Sally, quoting a popular song. "But do you realize, Doris Craig, what a different girl I've become since I knew and cared for *you*?"

She was indeed a different girl, as Doris had to admit. To begin with, she *looked* different. The clothes she wore were neat, dainty and appropriate, indicating taste and care both in choosing and wearing them. Her parents were comparatively well-to-do people in the village and could afford to dress her well and give her all that was necessary, within reason. It had been mainly lack of proper care, and the absence of any incentive to seem her best, that was to blame for the original careless Sally. And not only her looks, but her manners and English were now as irreproachable as they had once been provincial and faulty.

"Why, even my thoughts are different!" she suddenly exclaimed, following aloud the line of thought they had both been unconsciously pursuing. "You've given me more that's worth while to think about, Doris, in these three months, than I ever had before in all my life."

"I'm sure it wasn't *I* that did it," modestly disclaimed Doris, "but the books I happened to bring along and that you wanted to read. If you hadn't *wanted* different things yourself, Sally, I don't believe you would have changed any, so the credit is all yours."

"Do you remember the day you first quoted 'The Ancient Mariner' to me?" laughed Doris. "I was so astonished I nearly tumbled out of the boat. It was the lines, 'We were the first that ever burst into that silent sea,' wasn't it?"

"Yes, they are my favorite lines in it," replied Sally. "And with all the poems I've read and learned since, I love that best, after all."

"My favorite is that part, 'The moving moon went up the sky and nowhere did abide,' " said Doris, "and I guess I love the thing as much as you do."

"And Miss Camilla," added Sally, "says her favorite in it is,

" 'The selfsame moment I could pray,

And from my neck so free,

The Albatross fell off and sank

Like lead into the sea.'

She says that's just the way she felt when we girls made that discovery about her brother's letter. Her 'Albatross' had been the supposed weight of disgrace she had been carrying about all these fifty years."

"Oh, Miss Camilla!" sighed Doris ecstatically. "What a darling she is! And what a wonderful, simply wonderful adventure we've had, Sally. Sometimes, when I think of it, it seems too incredible to believe. It's like something you'd read of in a book and say it was probably exaggerated. Did I tell you that my grandfather has decided to purchase her whole collection of porcelains, and the antique jewelry, too?"

"No," answered Sally, "but Miss Camilla told me. And *I* know how she hates to part with them. Even *I* will feel a little sorry when they're gone. I've washed them and dusted them so often and Miss Camilla has told me so much about them. I've even learned how to know them by the strange little marks on the back of them. And I can tell English Spode from Old Worcester, and French Faience from Vincennes Sèvres,—and a lot beside. And what's more, I've really come to admire and appreciate them. I never supposed I would.

"Miss Camilla will miss them a lot, for she's been so happy with them since they were restored to her. But she says they're as useless in her life now as a museum of mummies, and she needs the money for other things."

"I suppose she will restore the main part of her house and live in it and be very happy and comfortable," remarked Doris.

"That's just where you are entirely mistaken," answered Sally, with unexpected animation. "Don't you know what she is going to do with it?"

"Why, no!" said Doris in surprise. "I hadn't heard."

"Well, she only told me today," replied Sally, "but it nearly bowled me over. She's going to put the whole thing into Liberty Bonds, and go on living precisely as she has before. She says she has gotten along that way for nearly fifty years and she guesses she can go on to the end. She says that if her father and brother could sacrifice their safety and their money and their very lives, gladly, as they did when their country was in need, she guesses she oughtn't to do very much less. If she were younger, she'd go to France right now, and give her life in some capacity, to help out in this horrible struggle. But as she can't do that, she is willing and delighted to make every other sacrifice within her power. And she's taken out the bonds in my name and Genevieve's, because she says she'll never live to see them mature, and we're the only chick or child she cares enough about to leave them to. She wanted to leave some to you, too, but your father told her, no. He has already taken out several in your name."

Doris was quite overcome by this flood of unexpected information and by the wonderful attitude and generosity of Miss Camilla.

"I never dreamed of such a thing!" she murmured. "She insisted on giving me the little Sèvres vase, when I bade her good-bye today. I hardly liked to take it, but she said I must, and that it could form the nucleus of a collection of my own, some day when I was older and times were less strenuous. I hardly realized what she meant then, but I do now, after what you've told me."

"But that isn't all," said Sally. "I've managed to persuade my father that I'm not learning enough at the village school and probably never will. He was going to take me out of it this year anyway, and when summer came again, have me wait on the ice-cream parlor and candy counter in the pavilion. I just hated the thought. Now I've made him promise to send Genevieve and me every day to Miss Camilla to study with her, and he's going to pay for it just the same as if I were going to a private school. I'm so happy over it, and so is Miss Camilla, only we had hard work persuading her that she must accept any money for it. And even Genevieve is delighted. She has promised to stop sucking her thumb if she can go to Miss Camilla and 'learn to yead 'bout picters,' as she says."

"It's all turned out as wonderfully as a fairy-tale," mused Doris as they floated on. "I couldn't wish a single thing any different. And I think what Miss Camilla has done is—well, it just makes a lump come in my throat even to speak of it. I feel like a selfish wretch beside her. I'm just going to save every penny I have this winter and give it to the Red Cross and work like mad at the knitting and bandage-making. But even that is no *real* sacrifice. I wish I could do something like she has done. *That's* the kind of thing that counts!"

"We can only do the thing that lies within our power," said Sally, grasping the true philosophy of the situation, "and if we do all of that, we're giving the best we can."

They drifted on a little further in silence, and then Doris glanced at her wrist-watch by the light of the moon. "We've got to go in," she mourned. "It's after nine o'clock, and Mother warned me not to stay out later than that. Besides I've got to finish packing."

They dragged the canoe up onto the shore, and turned it over in the grass. Then they wandered, for a moment, down to the edge of the water.

"Remember, it isn't so awfully bad as it seems," Doris tried to hearten Sally by reminding her. "Father and I are coming down again to stay over Columbus Day, and you and Genevieve are coming to New York to spend the Christmas holidays with us. We'll be seeing each other right along, at intervals."

Sally looked off up the river to where the pointed pines on Slipper Point could be dimly discerned above the wagon bridge. Suddenly her thoughts took a curious twist.

"How funny,—how awfully funny it seems now," she laughed, "to think we once were planning to dig for pirate treasure—up there!" she nodded toward Slipper Point.

"Well, we may not have found any pirate loot," Doris replied, "but you'll have to admit we discovered treasure of a very different nature—and a good deal more valuable. And, when you come to think of it, we did discover buried treasure, at least Miss Camilla did, and we were nearly buried alive trying to unearth it, and what more of a thrilling adventure could you ask for than that?" But she ended seriously:

"Slipper Point will always mean to me the spot where I spent some of the happiest moments of my life!"

"And I say—the same!" echoed Sally.

THE END